MW00563215

Ghosts of West Baltimore

David Simmons

Broken River Books

A Broken River Books Original
Broken River Books
Oklahoma City, OK

Copyright © 2023 by David Simmons

Cover art © 2023 by A.A. Medina

Interior design by J David Osborne

All rights reserved.

This is a work of fiction. All names, characters, places, and incidents ware the product of the author's imagination. Where the names of actual celebrities or corporate entities appear, they are used for fictional puposes and do not constitute assertions of fact. Any resemblance to real events or persons, living or dead, is coincidental.

ISBN: 978-1-940885-62-9

No portion of this book may be reproduced in any form without written permission from the publisher or author, except as permitted by U.S. copyright law.

Printed in the U.S.A.

*"The fastest way to get from Israel to Africa
is Park Heights Avenue"*

- Anonymous

*"I'll be seeing you
In all the old familiar places
That this heart of mine embraces
All day through"*

- Billie Holiday

1

AT DISCHARGE, THE HOSPITAL provided Worm with a wheelchair and a prescription for midodrine that he would need to take every four hours for the rest of his life. Not that he had much time left anyway. The radiation had destroyed his body on a cellular level and an especially nasty subconjunctival hemorrhage had blotched the sclera of his remaining eye red, making him look like an eastern box turtle.

"This is important," Dr. Osman said. "What's happened to you is, well, there's no precedent for it. I don't understand how you're still alive. None of my colleagues do. It probably feels like a bad sunburn all the time, maybe? That's how our cancer patients undergoing radiotherapy treatments describe it. We measure radiation in units called *grays*. Chest x-rays and mammograms are less than one of those units of measurement. You've been exposed to approximately eight grays. Six to twelve is somewhere in the lethal range but for some reason you're still here. You should have died weeks ago. I remember reading an article about a Russian double agent that ingested coffee with radioactive polonium and he received somewhere around eight grays, similar to you."

"What happened to him?" asked Worm.

"What?" Dr. Osman frowned. "He died."

"That's fucked up."

"You have to take this seriously."

Worm shrugged. "I'm trying. I really am. I don't have an amygdala anymore."

"I know this. I reviewed your imaging. Multiple times."

"It's like it's hard for me to worry about anything. Like, I'm not worried about what happens anymore. Like, what happens in general. I feel like parts of me are going away, or gone. I'm missing my eye, the amygdala, like I said, all kinds of shit, but still I'm not worrying. Even though those are important things. My things."

"You refuse to tell us what happened, so we can only help you so much."

"I have," Worm insisted.

"I'm not entertaining your mech suits and monsters and drug dealer stories. At this point, I don't even care. The radiation poisoning is the pertinent matter. For when you leave here. Back to the midodrine."

"Yeah. You were talking about me bleeding out of my skin."

"Not literally." Dr. Osman turned towards the computer monitor on the mobile cart next to her and tapped something on the keyboard. "But your internal organs and brain need blood and right now all your blood wants to do is run away to your skin and muscles. Another goal is to increase cardiac output."

"Still sounds like you saying I'm gonna bleed out of my skin and shit, doc."

There were the dexamethasone injections to keep him from going into shock. Something had happened to his adrenal gland during the fight with Mecha-Sweet Breath and the Arturo-Thing.

"I gotta give myself shots of this four times a day? That's what you saying? What about my quality of life?"

Dr. Osman frowned. "Quality of life? Without these medications you aren't going to have *any* life. All of this is to keep you alive. You have to take care of yourself when you leave here. We've been doing it for you. The state has been doing it for you and—"

Dr. Osman sucked her teeth and stopped talking. Worm had been in the hospital for over a week now. Dr. Osman was special. Long, black hair and thick thighs, defined calf muscles. Worm could see her shape under her pale blue scrubs. When she sat down her pants produced that crease between the hip and thigh, the place Worm's partner Marlon had referred to as *Thass*. When she would lean in and check his wounds he would catch a scent of lavender and baby powder, a scent that would make him stir but never do anything about the stirring.

Good for him.

He wasn't the type to hit on his doctor. And he knew better, too. She hated the fact that the hospital was devoting so much time to his expensive and experimental treatments. She hated his Medicaid coverage. Hated that she had worked so hard to save the life of someone like him. He was a criminal after all. He could see it in her look; the way the corners of her mouth always turned down slightly the moment before she spoke to him. How the line of her mouth gradually lifted up as she spoke about medicine and treatments and illnesses and things that she was passionate about. How it turned back down the moment she looked back at him. So he caught the scent when he could and was grateful for that.

Worm nodded at Dr. Osman. "I get it. I'm taking it seriously. It's radiation poisoning, but not because the radiation in my body is poisoning me, but because broken down bits of my body are floating around fucking my shit up."

Dr. Osman took her tortoise shell eyeglasses off and placed them on the mobile cart. "We really have done everything we can for you."

Worm thought about the potassium iodide treatments and the di-ethylenetriamine pentacetic acid that binded to the radioactive metals in his body then came out in his piss and shit, stopping the rest of the atoms in his DNA from ionizing. He thought about his cells dying, reproducing into defective cells that would inevitably die, or reproducing into defective cells that would continue replicating into cancer and on and on until it all consumed him.

"We've given you blood transfusions, antibiotics, stem cell trans-plants, and we've been successful in keeping you from getting new infections. It obviously helped since you're still alive. Despite all the damage, a lot of your cellular machinery is still working. But the cellular replication machinery is much more sensitive to radiation, and it will stop working eventually. You can live without your cells replicating for days or weeks. Parts that *do* need to replicate quickly to work correctly show the damage first."

"What about colloidal silver?"

"I beg your pardon?"

"Colloidal silver," Worm offered. "You know, like what they put in newborn baby eyes. You feel me? For the conjunctivitis and shit. I had a cell buddy who told me you can buy that shit online. That it cures hepatitis, diabetes, AIDS, all that. You just gotta drink it. And keep drinking it. Big Pharma just don't want us to know about it. So they can keep us sick. But they drink that colloidal silver shit in Uganda. My celly was Ugandan, he knew all about it. That's why they live forever, you feel me?"

Dr. Osman stared blankly at Worm.

"How do I know when I'm going to die?" he asked.

"If I'm not completely wrong, the last two days before you die, you will feel perfectly fine. But your body will not be working anymore in any way. Just using up its resources waiting for the first organ to collapse."

Worm took one of his dreadlocks between his thumb and index finger and twisted it around the knuckle, knotting it closer to the scalp. "That's fucked up."

"Yes," she said, taking out a tray with two syringes.

He twisted the lock around his finger tighter, imagining it coming out at the root without resistance. Eventually it would come out. Fall out.

Worm wasn't slow. He knew what radiation poisoning was. He knew it wasn't poisoning in the traditional sense. Radiation poisoning was a misnomer. That was just the name for the resulting symptoms after being hit with radiation. High energy subatomic particles connecting with your cell tissue. Like a microscopic version of Mecha-Sweet Breath's flechette rounds bouncing around inside of his body, tearing apart the molecules that made up his cells like tissue paper. It wasn't something that could be flushed out of his system. His system was fucked.

The police had come to question him more than once, and he had told them the truth, which only succeeded in causing more problems for him.

Initially.

At first, the detectives sent to talk with him hollered that they would charge him with obstruction of justice and conspiracy, that they would hit him with endless VOPs and stack up charges so high they would bury him under the jail.

And arson.

Definitely arson. They were going to pin the whole club fire on him. It had to be him. If it wasn't him, it still had to be.

And then they just *switched*, like some kind of command had been sent to their internal programming, causing their whole demeanor to instantly change.

There were two detectives; one black and one white. The black cop was tall and looked like broccoli. His hair rose from his head like a shaggy pencil eraser. He had a gold canine tooth that he revealed when he spoke by raising his upper lip in a lopsided sneer.

"I'm gonna be straight with you. I looked all up in your file and you're gonna die. That's a fact. Realistically, you got about three or four days. And I don't want to deal with this shit. Ain't nobody tryna do no paperwork, this or that, take a statement. Shit. I don't need to take your report if you're gonna die before it's time for you to stand trial. And you will. Die, that is. Understand?"

Worm sat up in his hospital bed. "Say less. I'm with it."

The white police spoke with an Eastern Shore accent. "I don't think you get how little I care about you. You probably did everything, all kinds of wicked shit. It's not that I don't got nothing to charge you with. We can do whatever the fuck we want. I damn sure don't mind telling you that. You think I give a fuck what you think? I do not give a fuck about those Greek gangsters or their aggressively flammable club. Self-cleaning oven. Understand? I do not care about what happened to them and I do not care what happened to you. As far as I'm concerned, things worked themselves out. What my partner is saying is that we're going to leave and forget about this and you're going to die. Nobody cares. Just make sure you die. It's extremely important that you die."

The white police was shorter than the black one. He wore a gray sweatshirt with the sleeves rolled up well past his elbows exposing brilliantly-colored tattoos of koi and lotus flowers. Pale blue eyes the color of ice water sat close together in the center of his moon-shaped face. His lips were thick and purple and squirmed against each other like mating worms when he spoke.

"You'll never see me again," Worm said.

And he had meant it. He had no intentions of ever dealing with these detectives or any kind of law enforcement.

The white cop looked at the black cop. Then he looked at Worm and hiked his pants up. "We're Detective Lieutenants, you know."

"Huh?"

The black police nodded. "That's right. Detective Lieutenants. Not just regular detectives."

"They sent both of y'all here? That seems like an overreaction."

The detectives smirked and said nothing.

"I thought Detective Lieutenants supposed to wear blue pants and white shirts with their ranks on their collars."

The white cop got up in Worm's face, close enough for him to smell the strawberry Chloraseptic spray on his breath. "We wear what we want, you fucking nonfactor!" he screamed. His baleful face darkened, the vein at his temple popping out and pulsing like the proboscis of a ribbon worm.

The black detective leaned in and put his hand on the white detective's shoulder. "Hey, hey. It's OK. He's a dead man. He's not worth getting all worked up over."

The white police licked his lips. "He really upset me."

"I know, Andrew, I know."

The black cop started massaging the white cop's shoulders. The white cop arched his back and whimpered. Worm, uncomfortable and unsure what to do, closed his remaining eye and tried to keep perfectly still.

Worm kept his eye closed until he heard the sound of the door slam shut. He no longer heard the sound of the white police moaning or the black police soothing him. When he opened his eye, they were gone.

"Are you listening to me?" asked Dr. Osman.

"Yeah, sorry."

"The meds should keep you going," Dr. Osman went on. "There's the granulocyte colony-stimulating factor to promote the growth of your white blood cells and counter the effect of the radiation on your bone marrow."

"That's the name?" Worm asked.

"What?"

"Granulocyte colony-stimulating factor?"

"Yes."

"That's a wild name."

"I already explained your dexamethasone injections, yes?"

"Yes," Worm said. "Four times a day."

The doctor nodded and typed something on the mobile computer station. "There's a man here to pick you up."

"The fuck?" Worm frowned. "Damn. I'm sorry. Who's here to do what?"

"Your ride. I think it's your probation officer. I don't remember what he said his name was. He's with VPI. He brought paperwork."

VPI was the Violence Prevention Intervention unit. Somehow, Worm had forgotten about probation officers. He would have one. He was supposed to have met his probation officer before everything went crazy in Greektown. Although he had made it to his placement on time, he had also died shortly thereafter. Just because they had zapped him back to life and that had happened days ago, and he had been a little busy recovering in the hospital after saving the Eastside, didn't mean the system would make an exception for him or forget he existed.

It seemed his probation officer had been in no rush to see him either, at least not until he had been released from Sinai.

"And take these," Dr. Osman said, holding out a plastic sleeve about half the length of a toilet paper tube. She removed the white sleeve, revealing a black sleeve inside that unrolled into a thin, translucent, gray material in the shape of a pair of sunglasses. "These are mydriatic sunglasses."

He took the disposable sunglasses from her and put them on. "This works. Thank you."

"We'll need to see you again in one week," she said. "You'll be able to see one of our other doctors at our Remington satellite location."

"I wanna see you."

The doctor frowned. "Don't do that. Be safe. Take your medicine. Your shots. Good luck."

A male nurse and a female security guard came around the curtain with a wheelchair for Worm. They got him in the chair and wheeled him out of the room while Dr. Osman went to see her next patient.

"Got 350 on me, it ain't bus fare"

- YG Teck

2

OLOMON TOOMP HANDCUFFED WORM and put him in the shotgun seat of his Malibu.

"You mine now, lor bitch," said Toomp. A white ball of spit formed on his bottom lip. "I own that ass. That's why I'm finna throw these bracelets on your bitch-ass every time I see you. I can make you eat off the floor. Like a dog. You hear that, doggy? Do what I want with you, when I want with you. You understand? Disobey me? You must be crazy, shorty. I can hit you with a needle full of that fetty, boa! I read your file. Dopefiend ass lor boa. I can hit you with a hot shot. When you not looking. They'll just think you went too hard. Hit you right here, fuck nigga."

Toomp pointed to his carotid artery.

When Oloman Toomp said the word *fuck* in the phrase *fuck nigga,* the *U, C,* and *K* came up from the pits of hell, and some kind of alchemy made it sound like he was saying the word *yuck* at the same time as he said *fuck,* disgusted and covered in thick phlegm the color and consistency of Royal Crown hair grease.

Oloman Toomp was less a man and more a deliberate assault, a force that swallowed up the life of everything around it. Like one of those sinkholes in Guatemala, but sentient, and terrifyingly capable of wielding the long dick of the law and fucking anyone he wanted with it.

Toomp tore the disposable sunglasses off Worm's face and tossed them out the open window. Worm watched the wind batter the sunglasses until they unfolded into a flat sheet that got carried up and away, flying through the air until he could no longer make it out against the pale, gray blade of sky. "You don't need that shit."

Worm hated Olomon Toomp already.

No, he didn't quite hate the man. He was just disgusted by him. Hate was a selfish feeling, and he didn't so much as care about what happened to himself anymore. The removal of his amygdala left him with a lack of strong feelings about anything, it seemed.

It wasn't just the fear that was gone. It was like seeing the world through a filter that gave everything blurred edges. Life seemed quieter, in a way. True, it had become difficult to recognize facial expressions, especially those associated with fear or stress, like he had lost a whole chunk of his emotional vocabulary.

But he could move slowly. He could figure it out.

Oloman Toomp was speaking again but Worm tuned him out.

When he was at Maryland Reception, Diagnostics and Classification Center years ago, he heard a skinny dope fiend from over East ranting about a sadistic probation officer and former Black Guerilla Family member with *2-7-6* tattooed under his eye.

Oloman Toomp.

Worm had never heard of a *former* BGF member. And you never saw any young ones either. He had been locked up with them and the older heads were militant.

At ECI, he was housed in administrative segregation with a BGF named Smiles. "BGF is not a gang," he had said. "Take from that what you will. It's not something that's openly advertised to the public. It's an unspoken loyalty that's not something easily validated by law enforcement. Nobody is going to tell you they are BGF. It's an *if you know you know* situation. It's about blackness and enterprise, you feel me?"

Smiles had been talking about how secretive BGF was while talking about BGF to Worm, an outsider. That amused him.

But there was no denying how serious they were. Back in 2015 when Freddie Gray was killed by the police, the BGF shot callers put an order out to the Baltimore drug gangs, telling them to stop their beef with each other and hit the police instead. And on the west coast, where they were initially formed, BGF went to war with the Brand, La eMe, the Bloods, Crips and pretty much the whole California Department of Corrections.

But it's hard to recruit when everyone is waging war on you and the prisons are locking down anybody with George Jackson books or memorabilia. None of the leaders were on mainline anymore; all of them spent the winters of their life sentences in the SHU.

But being one of the most powerful prison gangs was like having the best free state insurance when radiation was destroying your body at a cellular level.

He didn't know anything about that shit except for what he had been told. Baltimore was not a gang city. There was BGF, a prison gang that spread to the streets in many ways. That was pretty much it. Sure, there were scatterings—various sets of Crips and Bloods that had been set up and sanctioned by legitimate out of towners plugged in with Los Angeles—but Baltimore *was not* a gang city. The only gang that meant anything in Baltimore was BGF, which explained the reason for Oloman Toomp's legend having a Black Guerilla Family layer to it.

There was even talk that this probation officer was ex-military; black ops in Africa or something like that. How he would have found time to rank up in a prison gang and also do ethically murky wet work in banana republics and developing nations, Worm didn't know. He couldn't get the timeline straight in a way that made sense to him. For people to create such a mythology around the man, he must have been a wild boy.

And now he was his probation officer.

Toomp smashed Worm's face into the dashboard of the Malibu. "You daydreaming on me, lor boa?"

Worm touched his upper lip with the tip of his tongue and felt wetness. He wondered if his nose was broken. "I'm sorry."

"Don't be sorry!" barked Toomp. "You know who's sorry? Sorry-ass niggas. Sorry-ass niggas always sayin sorry."

Worm nodded and tipped his head back.

"This what you gon do," Toomp said, wooden matchstick between his teeth, the red head of it bobbing up and down as he spoke. "You gon check into this placement, understand? You gon check in and not give nobody no trouble and most importantly, you gon shut the fuck up."

Toomp put the car in drive and went south on Greenspring. The anxious energy of the hospital's entrance shrank in the rearview and the tree-lined streets and red brick, single family houses of Cylburn came into view. The arboretum passed by on their left.

Worm thought about Simone. He hadn't thought about her in a while. He decided that he wouldn't.

Toomp spat out the open window. "You know why you gon check in, mind your manners, and not say shit when you get there? Hold up bitch, I'mma tell you. It's simple. Because the greatest enemy of progress is *you* not shutting the fuck up. You feel me?"

Worm nodded.

"This placement you going to is called St. Ambrose." The red head of the wooden match bounced angrily between his nicotine-stained teeth. "This a special halfway house. For special motherfuckers."

Worm felt a tempestuous wave of nausea roll over him.

The radiation sickness.

A dizzying sensation that left him feeling as if his head were detached, a weather balloon floating in a cloud, his feet on the floor of car, arms leaden and unfamiliar, his true self disconnected from his body. The air around him thick and cloying. Each breath he took was a struggle, as if it were trying to suffocate him.

"These types of facilities do housing and support services for retarded niggas like yourself," Toomp continued. "Ex-prisoners with disabilities. Like I said: retarded niggas. They say you got fucked up, boa." Toomp looked Worm up and down, undressing him with his beady, Gila monster eyes. "You look fine to me."

Worm's head cleared and he felt somewhat normal again. A bit lightheaded, but decent overall.

Toomp made a right on Cold Spring Lane and the neighborhood began to change; the well-maintained homes giving way to dilapidated structures and boarded up storefronts, the bike lanes replaced with littered alleys.

Worm shrugged. "The doctors at Sinai said I got radiation poisoning."

Toomp turned and stared at him, his eyes like pools of black ice. Nothing but nefarious fuck shit in his unyielding gaze, no hint of warmth or anything human. It was a desire-based, animal-need, viscera-eating, teeth-grinding look. It was a look that seemed to last forever, and Worm couldn't help but wonder what the man was thinking, what was going through his sweaty, bald, brown head. And then, just as suddenly as it had begun, Toomp cut the icy gaze off and turned away, leaving Worm to stare at the *2-7-6* tattoo under his eye and wonder what the fuck had just happened.

"Radiation poisoning stupid as hell," barked Toomp. He took a key out of his shirt pocket and motioned for Worm to turn in the seat. "Ain't no radiation poisoning, for real. It ain't the radiation doing the poisoning, ya overstand me? That part done already. That's why it's stupid as hell. What had happened was, you got all these broken-down pieces of your body poisoning you. Cells and shit. *Your* cells. At the same time though, the organs that's supposed to be fixing your shit are all fucked up too."

Toomp removed the handcuffs. Worm massaged his wrists then fondled the syringe packs and vials of medicine in his pocket.

Toomp raised his upper lip in a sneer. "That's why they giving you all these antibiotics and shit. To keep you from dying from a bacterial infection while your cells are getting they life together. That shit dumb as hell. You know who get bacterial infections?"

"Huh?"

"Bitches. Nasty-ass bitches with fucked up pH balances. You dying from some female-type shit, for real. Radiation poisoning? Shit. You stupid as hell, boa."

"Why?" Worm asked, then immediately wished he hadn't.

Toomp looked at him incredulously. "Why? Fuck you mean, *why*? Cause radiation poisoning, see that there, that shit there for sorry-ass niggas. Only a sorry-ass nigga gon die from his own body poisoning itself. This shit here? This shit here's your body turning on you. Fuck type of man get betrayed by his own body? You gotta own this vessel." Toomp pounded his chest with an ashy-knuckled fist. "That's some retarded-ass, sorry-ass shit, right there."

Worm looked out the window and counted the potholes that dotted the street like sores. "I see what you saying."

"You don't see shit." Toomp got stuck behind a white Acura with five percent tints. He leaned on the horn and swung the Malibu into the right lane then jumped back into the left, nearly swiping the front end of the Acura. "If you actually could see shit you would be out here tryna reduce your neurotoxicity. That's why you a stupid bitch. All you need for real is some antioxidants and shit. Vitamin C, vitamin E, vitamin D, and riboflavin. Green tea and L-theanine. In Uganda, niggas drink colloidal silver, say it cleans out all the sickness. Shit like that. But you won't listen. Because you *don't* see shit. Like I said."

They drove the rest of the way in silence.

"Tell somebody you from Baltimore, guaranteed they gon crab us"

- Young Moose

3

WORM SUNK INTO THE seat of the Malibu and thought about the time he had woken up in the middle of the night, hopped in his 2010 cocaine-white Acura TL, raced to the IHOP on Pratt Street and ordered a stack of chocolate chip pancakes, excited like a little kid.

He had a girl with him that night, a thick joint with long box braids and big, gold hoop earrings. White gold fronts on the bottom row, made to look like fangs. The bottom row fronts made her look like a cute bulldog.

"Why are we here?" she had asked him.

"Yo I don't even know for real," he offered. "I just wanted some chocolate chip pancakes. Like from when I was young. Like my mother used to make when I was real little. So I had to go. You here cause you with me."

She shrugged her shoulders and looked at her phone.

The food arrived at the table; coffee for her and a stack of chocolate chip pancakes and Coke for him.

"Can I getcha anything else, hun?" the frail, elderly waitress asked.

Worm got to pouring maple syrup on his pancakes. "Nah. Thanks, hear?"

The girl–he couldn't remember her name now–she fucked around with her phone while he got to chopping up his chocolate chip pancakes and shoveling fluffy heaps of denatured and coagulated egg, milk and flour protein into his mouth, syrup pooling at the corners of his mouth and mussing up the whiskers of his beard and mustache.

Then he saw it.

It was in the pancake. It didn't look like a chocolate chip because it was only half of a chocolate chip but it was shaped like half of an oval and the oval was black like a chocolate chip but the oval had legs and it was only half an oval because he must have eaten the other half already.

He pushed the plate away from him, towards the center of the table.

"What?" Bulldog said, eyebrows arched but not looking up from her phone.

"Yo," he said.

"What, yo?" She was looking at him now.

He pointed at the pancake, at the half-eaten roach which no longer looked anything like a chocolate chip. How could he have missed it? Being too greedy, too eager. Always doing too much.

"And?" Bulldog asked. "It's a roach. So what?"

"Fuck you mean, *so what*?"

"Yo," she said, back in her phone. "It is what it is, shorty. You can't do nothing about it now. I'mma still fuck with you."

"Fuck you mean, I can't do nothing about it?" he said, dipping his napkin in his glass of water and wiping his mouth and tongue with it. "Roaches in pancakes is disgusting work. These motherfuckers gotta fix they shit. Fuck you mean so what?"

"They probably got big barrels of flour and powdered eggs and shit back there, in the kitchen," she said, rolling her eyes. "Big barrels or bins or whatever and roaches and other shit probably be falling out the ceiling and off the walls and landing in that shit. Probably get stuck inside and die. They ain't hurting nobody, for real."

"That ain't right, yo."

"What you gon do about it?" she asked. "Like, for real. You gon un-eat that half of that roach? You gon sue IHOP? Nah. You gon show the waitress and she gon tell you the meal is free and that's that. You might even leave her a tip because it ain't her fault and you a good dude, for real."

Bulldog smiled and showed her fangs.

"We here, bitch." Toomp had bucked a U on Park Heights Ave and pulled the Malibu up to the sidewalk that flanked the entrance to St. Ambrose. It was clear the building had once been used by the church, not just from the name but from the sacral architecture that peeked through the ADA-compliant modifications. Mixed in with the weathered, red bricks were stained glass windows and conical structures at each corner of the rectangular roof, with a much larger pyramid shaped spire in the center. The wide arch above the entrance seemed to loom over him like an evil eye. The probation officer reached over his lap and unlocked the car door. "Well, the fuck you waiting for? Get the fuck out. Check in to your placement. Do what you told. And always remember what I said."

Worm nodded.

"Nah, fuck that. What I say?"

"Umm," Worm fumbled.

"I said you gone shut the fuck up!"

"Right."

"Because the greatest enemy of progress is..." Toomp gestured for Worm to finish the aphorism.

"Because the greatest enemy of progress is you—" Worm repeated.

"Because the greatest enemy of progress is *you* not shutting the fuck up!" Toomp cried, smacking Worm in the back of the head like a disobedient child. "Not me. You!"

Worm shrugged out of the car like a wet bag of laundry. His body still felt like it was melting.

Toomp pulled the door closed before Worm could do so. "Radiation poisoning, my dick!" he spat. And with that, the psychopathic piece of shit with an online degree from Devry in criminal justice drove off into the sunlight of Northwest Baltimore.

"Dope so clean got the sniffers nose running / and if you owe me better wear a vest the whole summer"

- C Watt

4

AT ONE POINT, THERE were two major streetcar routes in Park Heights; one that ran along the Avenue and three crosstown lines on Belvedere Avenue. Retail and restaurants were propped up along the lines, the residential neighborhoods slowly following. Pimlico Racecourse, surrounded by entertainment venues and restaurants and hotels that no longer exist today.

By the Fifties, the neighborhood had been settled by Jewish immigrants from Reservoir Hill and further out, some coming from as far east as Jonestown.

The *white flight* exodus of the Fifties changed all of that.

The Jews fled up the Avenue. Upper Park Heights and Pikesville flourished while black migration picked up momentum. This northernmost part of Park Heights from Northern Parkway to Slade Avenue became colloquially known as Jew Town. Blacks from the inner city with the same dreams of escape made their way up the Avenue. Back then, moving to Park Heights was symbolic of upper middle class, black excellence, home ownership, the beginning of generational wealth and the like.

And then things changed.

Absentee owner-landlords jammed two or three families into homes that had been chopped up and modified, homes that only one family had lived in previously. Landlords quartered and sectioned the properties down further, jammed more families in and shut down the properties that weren't profitable, further increasing the need for housing. Repairs never happened, maintenance was neglected. Vacant units were broken into by children or converted into crackhouses when the Eighties came.

Reagan and the CIA did their thing and the neighborhood became overrun with an army of dope dealers and vagrants that hogged the phone booths and street corners. Check-cashing businesses continued to spring up like vampires poised to suck obscene percentages out of already inadequate paychecks.

The Park Heights Community Corporation was created to provide housing, sanitation and energy assistance to the poorest residents. The organization vowed to take on joblessness and the staggering 70% unemployment rate in the northwestern neighborhood.

Then the Park Heights Community Corporation was closed down following allegations of financial irregularities, which turned out to be flat-out fucking corruption. Federal money being used for cash advances and bogus office expenses and out-of-town trips.

Park Circle to Woodland became Down Bottom. Woodland to Belvedere did not get a name, but the drug rings and crews from Oswego, Violet, Shirley and Wylie World made a big enough name for themselves for their individual streets to ring bells. Everything from Belvedere to Northern Parkway became Up Top.

And all the while, Northern Parkway split the neighborhood like an atom in a nuclear reactor, separating Jew Town from the rest of Park Heights—the black part of Park Heights.

And when you stood on one of the northern corners of Northern Parkway you could see the difference. The shift. The trash and debris and vacant homes and abandoned vehicles were nowhere to be seen.

The liquor stores were replaced by synagogues and Jewish learning centers.

Something happened here.

The line stuck in Worm's head as he stood on one of those corners now, telling himself he should really get to his placement. Toomp was an unhinged psychopath. A rabid dog. It would be a mistake to play with him, disobey him.

The thing about people like Toomp—and boy did Worm know a lot of people like him—is that they do not feel bad after the flash. This was a critical thing to understand about them, for it controlled their behavior and operating system.

The *flash*, as it were, was not part of them, but a separate thing that existed neither before them nor after.

They could commit an act of violence and move it to the side, as if it was a previous iteration of themselves that committed the act, and they could view that previous iteration of themselves in a cold and detached way, devoid of any emotional effect or affect. It was the old version of themselves that had committed the awful act, if the act itself was even awful, that is. How could they possibly know? When they were committing the act it felt right. And now it was in the past.

Fuck it, he thought, and crossed the light. Stop by the 7-Eleven. Get something to drink. Look around before he checked in to that St. Ambrose place for broken ex-cons.

Worm walked down Park Heights Avenue. The heat of the day felt like it was burning into his remaining eye, causing him to squint and tear up. His body's act of betraying itself was like being flensed, peeled and decorticated, the ozone orange sun making it all the more painful.

A black spot appeared in the center of his vision accompanied by the sensation of a belt being tightened around his lungs. His breathing became labored, his throat dry. He shook with fever as sweat coated his back and bound his shirt to his skin. The black spot shrunk to the size of a pinprick and then Worm threw up. The sound of his vomit hitting the sidewalk rushed through his ears like wind in a conch shell and the acrid taste of his tongue made him retch again. He dry heaved, moving towards the street so he could lean on a neon orange traffic barrier. He tried to catch his breath but couldn't. Leaned over, tried to inhale through his nose, let the gravity or whatever it was help the oxygen get to his brain faster.

"Let me see your phone, yo." A young man, not quite a child but still a kid, was standing in front of him, hand out, talking to him. "My shit dead. Ain't got no charger and I need to call my mother."

Worm curled his lip up. "What?"

"Your phone, yo," the kid insisted. "Let me see it."

Worm remembered that he was still the only person in Baltimore without a phone. He had one in prison, but never after. He never obtained one during his stay at the hospital. How could he have made that happen? And he had only been out of the hospital for thirty minutes, less than that, probably. "Ain't got no phone," he replied.

"Mannnnnnn." The kid backstepped and clapped his hands together, looking around as if addressing an audience, stepping forward, then backstepping again. "You bluffin. Why you ain't just say no, yo? Why you gotta be lying and shit?"

"Nah, for real," Worm said. "I don't have one. I just got out the hospital."

"Fuck that got to do with not having a phone, dummy? They got a rule talkin bout you can't have a phone in the hospital? Where they do that at? That don't even make sense. How a nigga call 911 with no phone? I'm just saying. You coulda just said you ain't wanna let me use your phone. You ain't have to start bullshitting for no reason."

"I'm not bullshitting," Worm told him. "I don't even know why I'm standing here explaining myself to you like I owe you shit, shorty."

"For real, it ain't even that serious." The kid scratched the back of his head. "I probably wasn't gon call my mother anyway. I was probably gon go through your CashApp and send myself some money from your shit. So, you not letting me use your phone is probably a good idea, for real."

"I don't have a phone."

The kid squinted at him. "Why your eye missing, yo? Why it look like that? That shit nasty. You ain't got no Stevie Wonder shades you can put on? Ain't got no kinda eye patch? You think you Fetty Wap? You just gon walk around with that nasty-ass shit all exposed for everybody to see? You just gon rep that empty-ass hole in your face?"

"Chill, yo."

"I'm just sayin. You weird. Old weird-ass nigga. Probably don't even listen to no YG Teck. Nigga walkin around Park Heights and don't even know who YG Teck is."

"Who?"

"Teck, dummy. How you in the Heights and you don't know no Teck? That's disgusting behavior. I'm talkin *Flood Da City, Don't Get It Twisted, Active, Shootout.* All that. How you don't know no Teck?"

Worm couldn't believe he was having this conversation. "I don't know, yo. I'm not up to date with all these new rappers, for real."

"Teck ain't new. Maybe you the one who's new. Or maybe you just old as fuck. Old-ass nigga. Dummy ain't even got a phone. Probably got some primordial shit back at your house with a keypad on it. Old Alexander Graham Bell-ass nigga."

"A house phone?"

The kid ran around in small, concentric circles then came to a stop. "This nigga really is retarded," he said.

Worm didn't want to hurt the kid but his patience was wearing thin. "Move along," he said. "I ain't about to play with you right now, shorty."

"Oh ard," the kid said, walking away and then turning around and walking backwards so that he faced Worm. "I'mma move along or whatever. But as soon as you gone, I'mma move right back."

The kid turned around and started jogging down the street. *What the fuck?* Worm thought.

"I'm from the home of heroin, that 21229"

- Smash

5

OLOMAN TOOMP PULLED THE Malibu over on North Fulton Avenue and put it in park, letting the engine idle while he ran his tongue along the back of his front teeth. His eyes went low as he thought about the amount of paperwork he still had left to finish. New motherfuckers always required new paperwork, and he had a new motherfucker.

Worm.

That was what he went by anyway. It didn't matter. Not like Toomp would ever call him that asinine shit, hell, he'd never call him by the name his mama gave him either. He was just another face, a new motherfucker who would soon be an old motherfucker.

And who the fuck would have an alias like that?

Worm. That was a terrible name. Worms were stupid because the sun could paralyze them. No eyes, sure, but they could *see* with their skin. Too much light exposure and they can't move. Can't go back to their burrows.

Stupid-ass worms.

Toomp popped the glovebox and got out a leather Dopp kit. Inside of the black bag was a vape pen and a vial of clear, viscous liquid that moved sluggishly when Toomp took it out and flicked the side of it. He tapped the button on the pen three times to preheat the α-Pyrrolidinopentiophenone.

Back when he was stationed at Camp Lemonnier in Djibouti City, he had gotten a taste for chewing khat, tonguing the masticated leaf and stuffing it between his cheek and molars.

He missed the Horn of Africa.

Camp Lemonnier was the only U.S. military base on the continent, used as a hub for counter-terrorism operations in the region. A high fence topped with razor wire surrounded the base, guarded by heavily armed soldiers. The buildings were functional and utilitarian, with a sense of permanence, despite the harsh desert environment.

The base had a feeling of isolation, as if it were cut off from the rest of the world and Toomp loved that separation, that feeling of being a part of nothing.

And the living conditions were better than decent. Ample room and easy living in shipping containers with A.C. adapters to plug his shit in and a converter for certain things, like the cheap television he found in the base's swap shop. DFAC was lit. Pizza Hut, Subway and some other name brand chains he couldn't remember on post. Two gyms, decent ones, and five-dollar haircuts that weren't half bad.

The vape pen blinked red to indicate that it had finished preheating and Toomp took a long pull off of it. He held the chemical in, inhaled through his nose twice and then blew the air out like he was blowing out birthday candles.

You could get massages on base too. At least back when he was there.

At a hole-in-the-wall, happy ending-type place in Ilot Du Heron named Ebyan's Palace. But not happy endings of the sexual kind. It just looked that way from the outside.

The first time Toomp had tried to insinuate a request for a handjob he had been tied to two pieces of rebar, crossed at the center to create an *X*. The bouncers, or whatever kind of security they were, beat him unconscious and then woke him up to knock him out again.

Toomp had come back later that week and killed everyone in the massage parlor.

He let the memories wash over him as the α-PVP took hold. The way it felt to smack the head of his cock against the Habesha woman's face as he held the *jile* to her throat. The way the fear in her right eye made it look brighter than the left one, almost like a filter or cartoon effect, in a way that he could never understand as he ran the dagger back and forth across her throat, nearly sawing her head off.

He would have gotten the whole head off if it weren't for the other women walking in. He brutalized them also. Blood stained the white marble and gold accents.

It didn't feel as satisfying to remember the killing of the bouncers or security guards because he had decided to take them out from afar with an M24. Seeing their deaths from so far away made him feel nothing.

When he could get close enough to one of his victims, really get a good look in their eyes, that was when he could see it.

The autostereogram of their soul.

It always went in and out, that three-dimensional image of their true self. Like those Magic Eye paintings from the Nineties. Random patterns of multicolored dots that came together to form clear 3D images when you let your eye muscles go limp. How the image appeared to float above the rest of the painting.

That was what it looked like when you killed a person. When their shit came out of them.

At least that's how it looked when you let your eye muscles go limp.

Toomp hit the vape pen once more, letting his eye muscles go limp, then returned the works to the leather Dopp kit. He walked around to the front of the car and propped the hood up so he could double park without getting hassled. Thought about how clever he was for knowing that trick.

Not at all like the stupid bastard he was paying a visit to. And boy was he a stupid fuck. Toomp felt his manhood growing hard. His heart started racing as he approached the rowhouse.

Toomp knocked once.

Again.

And then he kicked the door in, his erection raging, beads of pungent sweat running down his temples. The air around him smelled of rotten apples and sickness. "Lights" by Journey played from somewhere beyond the living room.

Randy Bratzewski, Toomp's stupid, good-for-nothing, 3:00 p.m. home visit appointment, sat on the couch with a spoon in one hand and a lighter in the other. Toomp bolted over to Randy and smacked the spoon out of his hand, knocking over the coffee table and kicking up a cloud of cigarette ashes into the air. Randy's eyes widened to the size of dinner plates.

"You a stupid motherfucker, huh man?" Toomp sat down on the couch next to Randy. He wrapped his arm around the weaker man's shoulders and palmed his forehead with his massive hand.

"I'm sorry, I'm sorry," sobbed Randy.

Toomp flexed his bicep and tightened his grip on Randy's face. "Aw Lawd. Not another motherfucker out here tryna tell me how he sorry. You know I hate a nigga who always wanna say he sorry. My, oh my, how I hate him so. Tell me, Randy. Why do I hate a nigga who always wanna say he sorry?"

Randy looked down at his toes poking through the holes in his socks. "I don't wanna say it, Mr. Toomp. Please."

Toomp smacked Randy in the mouth with one hand and tightened the arm lock on his forehead with the other. "What you mean you don't wanna say it? I just told you to say the shit. Fuck wrong with you? I ain't gone tell ya again, ya overstand me? Now, why do I hate a nigga who always wanna say he sorry?"

Randy shut his eyes and shivered. "Because only sorry-ass niggas say they sorry."

It happened fast.

Toomp swung Randy up in the air and off the couch, then body slammed him through the turned over coffee table, cracking off a leg and shattering the glass top. "Oh yeah, bitch! It's on now. Cracker-ass, pussy-ass, peckerwood-ass whiteboy wanna say *nigga* like he down, huh?

"Please," Randy pleaded. "Oh God."

The probation officer got on top of Randy and started going to work up the sides of his head first, pummeling his ears until they lumped up like cauliflower. He put his thumb in Randy's mouth and pulled to the corner, tearing the inside of his cheek. "You ever been fishhooked lor nigga? That what that is. Nasty-ass bitch."

Toomp took his shirt off, balled it up and tried to stuff it in Randy's mouth but gave up when he couldn't get it to stay. He tossed the shirt aside and wiped his hands on his chest, smearing Randy's blood and mixing it up with his own putrid cathinone-sweat. He was out of breath but his erection was still drilling a hole through his jeans, the crotch of his pants pulsing with the beat of his heart.

Toomp rolled off of Randy and lay down beside him, resting his open hand on top of Randy's crotch. Randy froze and did his best to turn invisible, did his best to ignore the weight of the sadistic probation officer's hand as it rested palm down, gently overtop his dick.

Toomp sighed. "It ain't even gotta be like this. These visits could be on completely different timing. Completely different kind of energy, you feel me?"

"Lights" by Journey continued to play.

"You know this stupid-ass song was supposed to be about L.A. at first?" said Toomp.

Toomp curled his knuckles and probed Randy's genitals through the thin material of his sweatpants. Randy tried to think about how the last Marc train out of Penn Station to Union Station was at 9:35 P.M. and how that was such an unusual time for such an important train, and he thought about the cost per foot of MC cabling from when he had a little side gig doing electrical T and M jobs, and he tried to think about anything that wasn't Toomp's fingers tracing the head of his penis.

"Real rap, shorty. The lyrics was supposed to go *and the sun shines on L.A.* but my man Steve Perry ain't like the way that shit sound. So he switches it to *and the sun shines on the Bay.* San Francisco and shit."

Randy's heart was a Thompson submachine gun in his chest. "Well, that worked out for the best, with them being from San Francisco and all. Heh heh. Right?"

Toomp got back on top of Randy and straddled him. "Fuck you say, boa?"

Randy whimpered like a small dog.

"Don't be afraid to speak up now, nigga."

"Well," Randy began, "they were never from Los Angeles to begin with. The band, I mean. And like you said, Steve Perry didn't like the way the lyrics sounded with *L.A.* so they switched it to the *Bay* instead. And I was just saying that that worked out well because that's where Journey is from. You know?"

Toomp beamed at Randy, his plastic smile frozen in a permagrin.

Randy gulped. "So, yeah, it's kinda like when art imitates life and life imitates art, right?"

Toomp grabbed Randy by the throat and ripped out one of his iridescent gauges. The earlobe split into two sections, blood spurting out of the cartilage. Randy screamed while Toomp pulled down his zipper, freeing his engorged, uncircumcised member.

Toomp's knees pressed down on Randy's arms as he jerked his dick up and down, the head of it nearly touching Randy's torn earlobe.

"Lights" by Journey continued to play. *When the lights go down, in the city. And the sun shines on the Bay.* The almost gospel-like harmonizing of Steve Perry, Neal Schon, Gregg Rollie and Ross Valory put Toomp in a hypnotic state.

He jacked his erection faster, harder.

"Please, oh God!" screamed Randy, as Toomp shot ropes of cum into the open wound of his ear.

"Come to find out you ain't have no real in you / and when you told me that you loved me you had a pill in you"

- Young Moose

6

WORM WAS INJECTING HIS second 4mg vial of dexamethasone when a black Mercedes-Benz Sprinter Van pulled into the 7-Eleven and idled. Insects made chittering noises in the brush surrounding the parking lot. Newport signs and deals for dollar slices airbrushed the glass storefront. There was a beat-up Corolla and a late model Oldsmobile in the parking lot but they were empty, the drivers already inside the store.

The side door to the van slid open and a group of Jewish boys filed out; black slacks and white dress shirts, their long, twisted *peyot* swinging as they made their way to the entrance of the 7-Eleven. The door chimed as they entered the store.

"The Rebbe says that if anyone tells you that they know what *Olam HaBa* is like, then they are a no-good liar," said the first boy inside the 7-Eleven.

"But the Talmud speaks of *Gehinnom*," said a smaller boy.

"So what, Shlomo?" asked the first boy. "Why must you always be so dense on these matters? It speaks of a sort of hellfire, and even that is unclear. Anyone who claims with any degree of certainty that they know what *Olam HaBa* is or what *Gehinnom* is, is lying to you. How can we know until we get there?"

The children walked throughout the store picking up strawberry sour straws and cola gummies. A woman stood behind the counter turning the hot dogs and Jamaican beef patties. She greeted them with a warm smile. "Hello, boys."

The boys stopped talking long enough to smile and nod. "Hell is not the place of your stupid cartoons and shows," the first boy continued. "It is not for punishment. Hell is a great kindness from *HaShem*. *Gehenom* is a place where the *neshama* goes to be cleansed of the *aveiros* we commit during our lifetime. It could be avoided through *teshuvah* or being punished in *Olam Hazeh*, but most people will go there for a time. It is an opportunity. *Gehenom* is a way for our soul to be cleansed. Maybe it is not a hellfire. Maybe it is the great washing machine? You put your nasty underwear in the washing machine and the washing machine throws your tighty whities around and around and this washing machine, it beats your dirty underwear up and down and around, and maybe it hurts, but after the wash cycle is finished, your nasty tighty whities are clean? You can wear them again, no?"

"I see what you're saying," said Shlomo.

The rest of the children were younger than Shlomo and the boy he was speaking with. They ran around the store, playing tag, picking up things and putting them down, bumping into a woman standing at the soda fountain then apologizing profusely.

The first boy, the oldest one, opened the refrigerator and took out a Coke. "Now just imagine if *you* were your tighty whities. If somebody put you in a washing machine and tossed you around and around with scalding hot water. How would this feel?"

Shlomo said nothing and studied a bottle of Mountain Dew Code Red like he was trying to decipher the Code.

The older boy grabbed Shlomo's wrist. "I asked you how this would feel! Don't be such a *schmendrick*."

"I'm sorry, Arnon!" yelped Shlomo.

One of the other boys, chubby with his *kippah* off kilter, tugged at Arnon's shirtsleeve. "*Zei azoy gut*. Can I get more than one candy this time?"

Arnon pulled his arm away. "Ah! You're such a *khazer!* I'm surrounded by nothing but *schmendricks!*"

Shlomo and the chubby boy grinned at each other.

Arnon groaned. "Listen, please. I was trying to explain to you that if you were thrown in a washing machine and spun around and around, and drowned with dirty water and soapy chemicals, you would also feel like Hell, no? But only through this violent wash cycle could you ever be worn again."

The chubby boy raised an eyebrow. "Why would you wanna be in a washing machine?"

"Feh!" Arnon waved him away. "You are too young and foolish to understand any of this. Just get your one sweet—not two, *one* sweet—and get back in the van. *Du farkirtst mir di—*"

Worm was by the sodas and bottled waters, debating on whether he would go with an Arizona Sweet Tea or a Cherry Coke when the boy named Arnon froze mid-sentence. His jaw snapped open and extended to an impossible length, his eyes wild and watering.

The chubby boy walked towards the exit and then stopped suddenly. His eyes clicked back in his head and his body began to seize. Worm looked from kid to kid and saw that whatever reaction the little fat kid and Arnon were having was happening to all of the Jewish boys. Worm watched as each one opened their mouths, their jaws cracking as they stretched their mandibles wider until their chins tapped their chests.

The boy named Shlomo was the first to start attacking people. He dove over the counter and grabbed the woman standing behind the hot dogs and beef patties. Blood sprayed across the counter as the boy bit off the lower half of her face. The woman tried to scream, but without her lower jaw and tongue she sounded like she was drowning. He rolled away from the woman and tried to chew the mouthful of chin, causing himself to choke on the meat and bone when it proved too difficult to swallow.

Two more boys hopped over the counter and piled onto the woman, snapping at her like hyenas and spitting out chunks of flesh. Shlomo went back to the woman's body and pushed the other boys off. He sat on her chest, pressing his thumbs into her eyes and gripping the sides of her head with his thighs. With unnatural strength, he pulled away the sides of her skull and opened the woman's face like a blue crab. Worm dropped the Arizona Sweet Tea he was holding.

Did that boy just crack open a bitch's face? Worm thought. *The fuck is this?*

Worm closed his eyes and felt the dexamethasone and adrenaline combo course through his veins, the radiation sickness spinning around his insides. He ran over to Shlomo and uppercutted him off his feet. The boy landed on his ass and growled in a way that was more animal than human. Worm grabbed the cash register off the counter and raised it above his head. Shlomo shrieked like an injured fox as Worm dropped the register onto his face.

"Fuck is going on, yo?" Worm said. He was still unsure of what was happening in the 7-Eleven.

A skinny Jewish boy's jaw unhinged, revealing a maw filled with razor sharp teeth. The boy let out a deafening roar and charged him. Worm stuffed a Pringles can down his throat, stretching the elongated jaw further. The boy's skull cracked when it hit the floor and the sickly-sweet stench of blood filled the air

"Chill, yo!" Worm patted his pockets, making sure he hadn't damaged any of his medicine vials or syringes. He was good. For now. But if he kept fighting these kids he might lose his meds. And for some reason he wasn't ready to die yet. Some kind of selfishness or pride or last-minute self-preservation.

The chubby kid ran towards him and Worm stepped to the side, sending the boy hurtling into the bags of Doritos and Rap Snacks. Worm lifted his knee to his chest and stomped all of his weight into the kid's back.

He wiped his hands on his pants. "I'm not tryna be out here killing kids, man."

The boy named Arnon had started crab walking towards him, belly to the ceiling with his blue and white *tzitzit* dangling.Worm kicked him in the back, lifting Arnon into the air and sending him tumbling down the candy aisle. The boy sprung back up and advanced towards him. Worm grabbed a jar of Nutella off the shelf and broke it over the boy's head. Glass and brown hazelnut spread clumped up at the top of his *kippah*.

The chubby kid was back. He came from the side and grabbed Worm's head, sticking his soiled thumb in Worm's empty eye socket. Worm screamed and stepped backwards, then threw a right hook that sent the boy flying into a rack of Old Bay magnets and Maryland state flag hoodies.

Four more Jewish boys, their eyes wild and frothing at the mouth, approached him on all fours. Worm scanned his opponents, sizing them up and looking for an opening to strike. One of the children lunged forward and vomited blood onto the floor. Spots of the dark blood dotted and streaked the toe of Worm's boot like an intentional splatter paint aesthetic. He stepped back and squared up. One of the other boys rose from the ground and threw a clumsy punch which Worm easily dodged and countered with a swift kick to the child's right temple. Blood shot out of the boy's nose and he crashed to the ground.

The remaining three Jewish boys rushed forward in a group, attempting to overwhelm him. Worm's heart raced, adrenaline burning through his insides like jet fuel.

And yet, he felt no fear due to his amygdala being removed by the Greeks. It was an unusual sensation; to be energized, prepared for battle, aware of the threat that surrounded him, yet unable to feel any concern about the danger of the threat.

The children closed in on him, snapping their jaws and growling, their animal snarls growing louder as they advanced. Worm grabbed a cell phone charger display and swung it at the child trying to flank him on the left, striking him in the side of the head. The other two children were on him now, biting his exposed flesh and clawing at his shirt with their tiny hands.

Worm fought fiercely, using the long cell phone charger display like a two-handed great sword. He swung the metal fixture wildly, striking one of the children in the throat and causing him to shuffle backwards, his hands gripping his neck, eyes wide and bright.

The other child was already upon him. He mule-kicked the boy behind him and threw another punch at the boy in front of him, aiming for the same area of his throat that he had already injured. Worm turned around right as the remaining child leapt towards him, teeth bared, pink saliva dripping down his bloodstained chin. Worm was too fast for the injured boy. He swung the fixture at the child's head, knocking him unconscious.

Worm stood panting and sweating, his heart banging against his ribcage, surrounded by the destruction of the 7-Eleven and the people inside it. There were bodies everywhere, most of them the Jewish children. The bodies of two employees were behind the counter, one slumped over the area where the register was before Worm smashed it over the boy named Shlomo's head. The patron who was using the fountain drink machine lay in a pool of spilled coffee, the cup still gripped tight in her hand. Bite marks tattooed the exposed skin of her arms and legs.

Worm studied his own arms.

Most of the bites on his body appeared to be superficial, but one of them looked nastier than the rest. Deeper. Worm could see the white meat shining through the openings the child's teeth had left in his forearm, the skin around the wound already turning an angry shade of red.

He stumbled out of the 7-Eleven and into the street, looking for help.

"Heard he got security now he hired to protect him / I just loaded up these .223's in this FN"

- Getum Verb

7

OLOMAN TOOMP PUSHED THE Malibu down North Fulton Avenue, the drying nut in his briefs causing his dickhead to congeal to his inner thigh. He rubbed his crotch through his jeans until he could peel his meat away from his leg. He lit a Newport 100 and inhaled deeply. Let the smoke out his mouth without exhaling and then vacuumed it back up through his nostrils.

A french inhale. That's what his daddy used to call them.

"Bitches love that shit," he would say. "That's how ya get em, ya heard me?"

Toomp's father came up to Baltimore from the primal muck and mud of Shreveport, Louisiana and used to say *ya heard me* all the time. That was his thing. One of his many things. Like the Newport 100s he smoked. The cigarette that Toomp was smoking now, french inhaling and such. *Cadillacs* were what his daddy used to call them.

"Watch this here," his daddy would say, placing a Cadillac between his index and middle fingers, with his thumb on the opposite side of the cigarette. He pushed the cigarette up and over his index finger with his thumb, rolling it across the back of his hand. When the cigarette reached his pinky finger he would tuck the little finger in, then push the cigarette back over his hand with his thumb.

Toomp took a left on Reisterstown Road and kept going. He made another left onto the Gwynn Falls Parkway and passed Mondawmin

Mall on his right. Douglass High School—the second-oldest high school in America created specifically for black students—went by on his left until he made a U-turn at the intersection of North Warwick and came back towards the high school.

He pulled off the Parkway and drove around Douglass and another building until he found a secluded spot under a tree next to a dumpster that he could back his car into.

The α-PVP was fucking with him, making everything too sharp and clean. The whites were all too white, the blacks not black enough, the shine of the sun too much like the amber urine of a sick person. It was too much. Too much stimuli. Too much color. He needed to disconnect. Bad. His heart was beating too fast and his dick had shrunk. He had unzipped his pants to study it as soon as he pulled over. A little snail on top of a shriveled sack.

He would have to do something about that.

Toomp took out the leather Dopp kit once more, this time unzipping the bag and producing a nasal spray bottle of 2F-ketamine and a shot glass. He dug into the bag and came back with a syringe and a small bottle of coconut oil which he placed on the passenger seat. He sprayed his dose into the shot glass then used the syringe to suck up 4ml of water out of the Deer Park bottle that had been rolling around the footwell. He sprayed the water into the shot glass and stirred it with the syringe. He sucked up the diluted chemical into the syringe and then placed it on the dashboard.

Toomp waited for a Honda Civic that was circling the parking lot to pass before he opened the bottle of coconut oil and started lubing up his asshole. When it seemed slippery enough, he grabbed the syringe off the dashboard and leaned forward, pulling the back of his pants down and plunging the syringe up his anus. His little snail dick got hard immediately, tripling in size, a massive slab of granite straining against his jeans. He pressed the plunger down and inhaled sharply.

"Yeah, bitch," he said, the 2F-ketamine making its way through his rectal blood vessels.

Now it was a race against time. He would masturbate in the car with the seat leaned back and try to cum before the dissociative took hold and tranquilized him into oblivion. It was a game. A fun one. Sometimes he would wake up with his dick out, his dopp kit and tools on the seat beside him. Other times he would cum before he lost awareness of self, and the post-nut clarity always seemed to make the ketamine high more introspective.

If Oloman Toomp was anything, he was an introspective mother-fucker.

"It's me again, same kid from Bentalou and Riggs / used to stay catching drama under Lafayette bridge / food stamps helped us keep a lor food in the fridge / ribs touching like lovers so you know what I did"

- Mullyman

8

WORM WIPED THE BLOOD and Nutella off his face and tried to figure out what to do next.

He was a collage of blue and yellow bruises, like little badges of honor, little medals for surviving another day in this fucked up city. The bruises were reminders that even though he had a hole in his head where his amygdala should be, even though he feared nothing, practically felt nothing, the bruises were reminders that he was still human, that he was flesh and blood and could still feel pain.

And of course, as usual, there was no one to provide aid, no one to help him, no one to ask for assistance. Worm watched the people in the street walk by, their heads down, mesmerized by the glowing screens in their hands. Passing by the acts of extreme violence and depravity as if they were nothing more than shadows on the red brick and glass storefronts. Eternally consumed, forever focused on chasing that next hit of dopamine from a notification or a like.

A procession of high school children marched by, their footsteps mixed with the sounds of digital chatter, a symphony of disconnection from the reality around them. Worm turned around and faced the 7-Eleven. The storefront was splattered with blood; spots and streaks in all directions that formed jagged lines and drips that ran down the window glass. In some areas, the blood had formed pools, congealing on the surface of the glass, while in others, it had begun to dry into rust-colored smears. And the blood was not merely splattered, but sprayed, a frenzied dance of destruction that tattooed the glass in an angry red tapestry.

He turned back towards the school children.

They ignored the canvas of violence that covered the storefront of the 7-Eleven, didn't notice the man with one eye, covered in blood and viscera, standing outside of the store. Never even looked in his direction. They were like little automatons with their robotic movements, swiping and scrolling and laughing while never looking up from their phones.

The children turned right on Northern Parkway and then Worm saw him.

One of the Jewish boys had made it out of the 7-Eleven and was limping up Park Heights Avenue like a broken puppet. Blood matted his hair and stained his *kippah*.

Worm decided to follow him, his actions driven by the need to play hero. Always putting his nose in other folks' business, always trying to play Superman. Like he was addicted to the rush of saving the day. He could never resist the urge to insert himself into the problems of others, even when it wasn't his place, putting himself in harm's way when he should have been checking in to St. Ambrose and *shutting the fuck up* like Toomp told him to.

He knew his actions were admirable, if not misguided.

He knew he needed to get to the new halfway house before that unhinged psychopath of a probation officer violated him and got him sent back up the road.

But still he persisted, following the boy up Park Heights Avenue to the big stone building with the Star of David above the double-door entrance. Maybe it was the way he saw himself, an empty vessel, aimlessly floating through life. Hollow. Adrift in a sea of insecurity and self-loathing, always feeling like he wasn't worth it, like he had to prove that he was worthy of love, of belonging. Maybe he thought he could prove his worth by being a savior.

Or maybe, he just couldn't resist the thrill of conflict, always wanting to be up in the mix of some shit, even when he knew it would destroy him.

Especially when he knew it would destroy him. Because that was the whole point, wasn't it?

"What's up, stupid-ass nigga?"

Standing in front of him was Sweet Breath—disgusting, larger than life and impossibly alive, the psychopathic drug dealer with one foot and rocket launchers mounted to his gargantuan mech suit, obese, dripping sweat and completely out of his mind.

He had died in the fight with the Arturo-thing, in his last breath telling Worm to follow him on Instagram.

"You waxing poetic?" the fat piece of shit asked. "Feeling sorry for yourself in that little self-involved way you got going on?"

It must have been a side effect of the medicine. Or the radiation poisoning. All the different changes happening inside of him. "You're not really here," Worm said.

"You always in the mix." Sweet Breath waved a mechanized arm. "All up in the next man's shit. Captain Save-a-Ho. That's you. Why you always tryna save the world for, Captain Save-a-Ho?"

"Somebody gotta do it."

"Somebody gotta do it," Sweet Breath mimicked Worm. He crossed his eyes and stuck out his tongue, the mech suit making hydraulic air noises as he wiggled his fingers behind his head. "You sound stupid as shit. You don't hear yourself? Why you think nobody else do it? Why you think nobody else out here tryna save the city? Think about it. Because it can't be done, motherfucker. You think you the first to try?

And I don't mean Baltimore. Baltimore no different from nowhere else. It's just a city. I don't care what nobody say. Everywhere just as bad as everywhere else because everywhere got people in it."

The lunatic had a point. Worm scratched the orbital bone around his empty eye socket, pointed at Sweet Breath. "What's it like being dead?"

Sweet Breath's face twisted up like somebody shit in his grits. "What's it, yo, I know this dumb motherfucker ain't just ask me what it's like being dead. How the fuck I'm supposed to know? I ain't no ghost. Ain't no such thing as ghosts. After this, it's just rot. I'm a figment of your imagination. A hallucination, you dummy. I can't tell you nothing you don't already know from knowing it. Dumb motherfucker. Look, right. This the part of the vision quest where you have your vision. I'm your vision! You stupid bitch. Fuck wrong with you? Get your life together. Listen to what I'm sayin. Sometimes you gotta go into a situation like you only got one bullet left, and you gotta ask yourself, is this what I wanna shoot at?"

And with that, the Sweet Breath mirage began to lose solidity, the image flickering like a faulty parabolic fixture until it evaporated and was replaced by the empty sidewalk and plastic red top vials of Park Heights Avenue.

"Park Heights, city life and vial stores / sub shops, kingpins and much more"

- Sac Banga

9

Toomp had his dick out when he saw her. And he had been really going at it too. The windows were all fogged up and the car reeked of fish and leaking batteries.

There was nothing he could do. He didn't have tints on the windows of the Malibu. And she was wearing black leggings, yoga pants or whatever they want to call them nowadays. Athleisure. Shapewear. Cream-colored, hooded sweatshirt that couldn't hide the curves of her body.

Toomp was out of the car with his dick in his hand, big globs of spit in the corners of his mouth and beard. The woman screamed and pushed something into his chest which sent lightning and jackhammers and underwater welding through his central nervous system. He fell to the ground, his dick still hard, a lightning rod standing up straight and pointing at the woman like an accusatory finger as she tased him.

"Stupid bitch!" the woman yelled, twisting the taser into his chest. "I'll fucking kill you. Eat it. Eat it, bitch."

Toomp felt his teeth chatter while his insides burst into blue flame. Every muscle in his body seized up as 80,000 volts of electricity ran through his being. His heart rate shot through the roof as he thought about everything and nothing at once. One of his lime green Foamposites went flying off as his right leg kicked in the air uncontrollably. The air smelled like electrified oil.

"What the fuck!? the woman screamed. She pulled back and stepped away. The electric crackling of the taser stopped. "You sick fuck!"

And then she was kicking him in the face. Over and over. Because Oloman Toomp had climaxed while she was electrocuting him. Long ropes of ejaculate splattered the sleeve of the arm she'd used to put him down.

So she continued to kick at his face. She kicked him in the chin. She stomped downward on his cheek when his face turned. She kicked him in the genitals. And less like a kick and more like a battering ram, she swung her leg at his upper body so that her shin and foot made contact. She swung again. She swung and kicked until Toomp was unconscious.

"I made a living with crack out / I made a vacant a crack house"
-Lenwood

10

It was dying when he saw it.

Or rather, in the process of killing itself.

Worm knew what it was from the black gimp mask with the zipper mouth. The matching black bodysuit, the metal rings seemingly placed at random with no sense of order or purpose. The empty eye socket behind the eye opening. The lone, remaining eye, the vacant stare with nothing human left in it. The zippered mouth opening like a crooked wound, slightly drooping in one corner erotically.

The Antiochian hunched over and retched up a thick spray of bloody vomit.

"The fuck, yo?" asked Worm. The gimp was running a cheese grater over his forearm. There was a large wound exposed through the torn suit. He rubbed the cheese grater back and forth, shredding leather and flesh.

The gimp looked up with one bloodshot eye. "Without purpose I'll still have purpose. As *art*. I will become art. The art *and* the artist."

The Antiochian ran the cheese grater up and down its arm. Worm watched the strips of flesh flutter to the ground as they fell out of the open end of the grater.

"How's that working out for you?" asked Worm.

"It's like, well, look. I'm going to bleed to death, right? And then somebody is gonna report the body and the police will come and then curious people will come and take pictures, right? And they'll see how fucked up I am and how crazy I look and then that shit will be everywhere. The artist and the art. I'll go fucking viral."

"No you won't," Worm said, watching the Antiochian cut itself, then turning to watch the bloody Jewish boy shamble off towards a gray, nondescript building with a large, steel statue of a menorah in front of it. "Nobody cares. This is Baltimore."

The Antiochian laughed.

Worm sucked his teeth. "Why aren't you out there hurting people? Or whatever it is y'all do."

"Aw man," the Antiochian said, gesturing to its legs. "I totally would be if I could. I'd much rather be fucking up other people instead of sitting here fucking myself up. But yeah, man. My legs don't work."

"The fuck?"

"Yeah, dude. My legs don't work because I got shot in the ass. Like, just recently. Or, I thought I got shot in the ass but maybe the bullet actually went a little higher, like through my back or something, I guess? My spine, maybe? So now I can't walk, you know?"

"What about your folks?"

"Huh?"

Worm looked around. "Your peoples. Your gang. Your squad. The rest of you clowns."

The Antiochian tapped the side of his forehead above the empty eye socket. "Hopefully fucking some people up. Like, I said, I'd much rather be hurting someone else, rather than myself. I'm sure that's what they're out there doing. I know that's what I would be doing if my legs were working."

"Whatever." Worm watched the injured Jewish boy limp up to the building entrance and nearly collapse. Before the boy could knock, the doors swung open and he was ushered inside the building by two muscular men in black hats. "What is that place?" Worm pointed.

"The Ellenbergen Center."

"The fuck is that?"

The Antiochian put the cheese grater down and tugged at a thin strip of flesh. "It's like a community center for Jews. But the *real* religious ones. The ones that be dressing like Hungarian peasants. You know who I'm talking about. They tryna promote Jewish awareness, knowledge and practice through outreach programs within the community."

The injured Antiochian said the last part like he was reading it off a pamphlet.

"I just fought a pack of Jewish kids, booted up on some kind of superhuman drug in the middle of a 7-Eleven, and then followed one of the fuckers back here. He went into that building. I've had it up to here with these wild-ass new drugs, yo. Their jaws opened all the way up, I'm talking *all* the way, like crocodiles. How's that for an outreach program? I ain't never seen no shit like that."

The Antiochian sniffled. "Right. The Rebbe."

"The fuck is a Rebbe? That's the name of the new drug?"

"Not everything is drugs, you know? It always seems like it is, but sometimes it's not. There are other things in this city, you know?"

"OK. Whatever. What's a Rebbe?"

"The Rebbe. He's the leader of their little Hasidic dynasty. Thinks he's the Moshiach."

"Moshiach?"

"The messiah."

Worm sighed. "Right. Of course."

"He's building an army of child soldiers. He has advanced biotechnology and living weapons that he commands. He's like, really dangerous and you can't do anything about it. Look, right, he's perfected this surgical procedure where he can—"

"I don't give a fuck about none of that, yo," Worm cut the Antiochian off. "Just tell me what the end game is."

"To usher in the World to Come? The End of Days? I don't know. I know he's been really emphatic about wanting to raise the dead. I know that. To put together an army. That's fucking wild. Crazy, right? Imagine having that kind of power. If you could do that, well, like, imagine if you could reanimate your dead enemies and then, like, rape them and torture them and kill them again and shit. And then you could keep doing it to them. Over and over. Just raping them and killing them and bringing them back and doing it again and again. Could you imagine? That would be so cool. He's probably not doing it for that specific reason. Well, I don't think he is. I would. I definitely would do it for that reason. Maybe he's doing it for art."

"Here you go. Art. It's always about that art shit with you sick motherfuckers."

"Yes," the Antiochian replied. "Everything is art. Art is everything."

"This shit ain't art." Worm pointed at the Antiochian's mutilated forearm. "And neither is this rabbi's shit."

"Rebbe."

"Whatever."

The Anitochian shrugged its shoulders and continued grating itself. "People will always have disagreements on what constitutes art. This is because of the pivotal role art plays in defining our values."

"Putting a cheese grater to your shit ain't art, yo. Nobody would agree with you about that shit. I'm talking about this rabbi or Rebbe or whatever. What's the point?"

"It's not your fault you don't get it. You're an idiot."

Worm shook his head. "Because I don't think violence is art, that makes me an idiot? Or what? Because I look and talk the way I do, I'm ignorant? Let me tell you something good: people say there's no good or bad art because that shit is subjective. That same bullshit has been drilled into folks' heads for so long that motherfuckers are incapable of aesthetic judgment that doesn't end up dissolving into relativization and nothingness. And what is art without judgment? So yeah, OK, cutting yourself is art. Whatever. But is it good art? Is it meaningful? Beautiful? What is it saying? Will it live forever? Fuck no."

"We're just going to have to agree to disagree."

"Fuck you. I don't have to agree with you about anything."

"You're missing an eye, talking to a paralyzed serial killer in a gimp suit on the corner of North Rogers and you just beat up–and most likely killed–a group of small Jewish children."

Worm remembered something that had been bothering him. "Yo, the fuck is an Antiochian?"

"I don't know," it said, working the cheese grater deeper into its arm. "We're from Antioch or something."

Worm scratched the back of his hand. "Like in the bible?"

The Antiochian's mask stretched wide as he smiled, his remaining eye sparkling. "Maybe."

"Fuck it." Worm grabbed the Antiochian's head and twisted until he heard its neck snap.

"Play me like a bitch, you gone hear them gun sounds / we don't do no drive-by's, we get out and we park now"

- OMC Ant

11

THE REBBE STROKED THE boy's shoulder and muttered a prayer under his breath. "...*shehecheyanu, v'kiy'manu, v'higiyanu laz'man hazeh.*"

A clear length of tubing, an inch in diameter, ran from the top of the boy's skull and up through his *kippah*. The rest of the tubing hung down the back of the chair the boy sat in. The Rebbe lifted the tube and attached an oversized hypodermic needle to the end of it. In between the boy's legs was a platform with a red button. The Rebbe stuck the needle in his arm and pressed the button. A gray liquid began to creep out of the boy's skull and up through the tube.

"*Oy vey,*" squeaked the Rebbe, his eyes rolling back in his head as the child's endogenous DMT passed through his blood-brain barrier. He pressed the red button once more, then fell into his Herman Miller lounge chair. He gripped his thighs and panted like a golden retriever.

The boy was awake. He stared off into the distance, his left eye squinting, as if he were skeptical of something. But he said nothing as the viscous, gray liquid left his skull.

The Rebbe was transported to a world of vibrant colors and shifting patterns and fractals. Every time, the chemical took him to a world beyond words, a divine temple of pentagonal gyroprisms and shimmering dodecahedrons. He felt weightlessness. He heard the distant sound of the kudu shofar, a low rumble that seemed to come from the heart of the earth.

"Mordechai!" yelped the Rebbe. "Come here please, Mordechai."

A boy, older than the one with the tube in his head, entered the room. He was dressed in a black double-breasted *rekel* that reached his knees, a worsted wool formal vest on top of his *tzitzis* on top of a white button-up shirt, and black and yellow basketball sneakers.

The Rebbe was staring at his shoes. Mordechai felt his face grow warm.

"What are *those*?" said the Rebbe.

Mordechai looked down at his Thunder 4s. They were black sneakers in the silhouette of the Air Jordan 4, originally released in 1989, but this iteration had the smooth black nubuck and the contrasting yellow accents on the eyelets, quarter panel, and internal tongue. The woven Jumpman emblem on the molded heel panel. The Air sole unit tucked away in the heel of the yellow polyurethane midsole.

These sneakers were his only indulgence. They were *everything* to him.

The Rebbe closed his eyes and exhaled through his nose. "I'm disappointed in you, boychik. For our people, clothing is not for boasting. We should be modest, yes? A person should not feel that he is something special. *HaShem* does not want this for us. The clothing, it does not make the man. The man makes the clothing."

"I'm sorry," said Mordechai, hanging his head. He was stupid for buying such flamboyant sneakers.

The Rebbe opened his glassy eyes again and glared at the boy. "If you're sorry, Mordechai, then why are you still wearing them?"

Mordechai felt a lump growing in his throat. He pressed the toe of his right sneaker against the back of his left sneaker and kicked the left shoe off. He sniffled and kicked off the right.

"You're looking at this wrong." The Rebbe removed the syringe from his arm and draped the tubing over the catatonic boy's shoulder. A gray drop of liquid beaded at the end of the needle. "Our style of dress is a uniform. *Tzniut.* You know this, yes? The *kapoteh,* the *shtreimel*—they make one aware that they are a part of a particular group, with its own set of values, customs, and rules."

Mordechai fixated on the Rebbe's last sentence. *With its own set of values, customs, and rules,* he thought.

Rules.

How was it acceptable for the Rebbe to do what he was doing? Getting high off the boy's naturally occurring chemicals.

But Mordechai knew that when it came down to it, it was a *halachic* question. To an Orthodox Jew, the question came down to whether it followed the dietary laws.

Was it kosher?

Milk from the body was kosher. And the Rebbe seemed to benefit from it. The Rambam himself had said that eating things from which the souls of most people are revolted—food and drink mixed with vomit, feces, foul discharges, or the like—were not kosher, but the Rebbe was certainly not revolted by it.

Mordechai was not revolted by it. The session would end with the boy unharmed. Sure, the child would need to sleep for a few days to recover, but otherwise he would leave unscathed and in good spirits. No harm, no foul.

Could it be made holy?

It had been previously decided that stopping an epileptic from having a seizure was a holy purpose for cannabis. Could the endogenous DMT coming out of the other boy's brain serve a holy purpose as well?

The Rebbe did not speak about this practice. Mordechai had no way of knowing the Rebbe's intent. Perhaps he received prophecy with the assistance of this act. He had never asked. Mordechai had never been instructed to blindly accept anything the Rebbe did, anything anyone did. Judaism was not a religion of blind acceptance. Questioning, doubting, these were not prohibited things. He could question, if he so chose.

But he did not.

Had it caused the Rebbe to become a *baal taivah*?

Mordechai saw the Rebbe as an ambitious man, a passionate man, larger than life, but he would never view him as someone controlled by their desires.

Was he committing *chillul HaShem*? Was he embarrassing His people, making a fool of God in front of the Jews and the *goyim*?

Certainly not.

Rabbi Amram Menachem Tzvi was a pillar in the Upper Park Heights community, loved by all from Slade to Northern Parkway, from Twin Ridge to Quarry East, from Glen to Cheswolde. He was a *tzaddik*. He would never be perceived as a buffoon, an embarrassment. Quite the opposite. What he was doing, with the boy and the chemicals and the needles—it wasn't shameful. This use, this resourceful utilization was not equal to a room full of *Yeshiva* boys laughing hysterically at the *Talmud* because they're all tripping on acid, the effect of the psychedelic making a mockery of holiness.

Mordechai considered all of this.

The Rebbe had so much responsibility, so much weight on him, so many people depending on him. What could a teenage boy possibly know about that? There were no shortcuts, no running before you walked, Mordechai knew. But they were living in the messianic age, right? Anything could happen.

Let's say the chemicals did change the Rebbe's state of mind to the point of dysfunction and embarrassment, Mordechai thought.

He recalled that the *gemara* said that when the temple was destroyed, prophecy was given to children, dogs and the insane. So even if it did change the Rebbe's mindstate to the point of insanity, perhaps in the depths of his madness he would find prophecy.

Besides, it was kosher.

And who was Mordechai to question him?

"Watch out for the big girl"

- Jimmy Jones

12

ONCE UPON A TIME, Worm had a mother. She was beautiful and she was made of honey and goodness and her name was Nikki.

In a time before the destruction of the tower, Nikki and young Worm lived in West Baltimore, high up in the clouds in a vertical village called Lexington Terrace. The mountain was made of gray stone and iron and it shot up into the sky and then disappeared into the heavens above. Knights in shining armor with M4 and M16 carbine rifles patrolled the walkways, pointing their weapons down at the peasants below and nodding at each other reassuringly.

Nikki wore black nail polish and loved the dissonant vocal melodies of Poly Styrene. She wore oxblood Dr. Martens and X-ray Spex concert T-shirts. Nikki made Worm try interesting foods before they were popular, like sushi and sea moss.

But sometimes Nikki was just so sad, and nothing, absolutely nothing in the universe, could make poor Nikki better when she got like that.

Nikki survived her first suicide attempt, an entire bottle of Xanax swallowed, only to end up throwing herself off the ledge of her eleventh floor balcony days later, which in turn, she survived as well.

Her jaw had split down the middle. Four of her ribs were broken and a nerve in her back had been severed. Her L3 exploded. She had fallen on her left side so her left arm no longer functioned. Broken left ankle and big toe. There was no explanation for why Worm's beautiful mother survived this fall.

And eventually the Matildas came for her.

They came on a Sunday morning, dressed head to toe in pale white cloth. The citrus undertones of their robes sparkled in the sun and contrasted with the grayness of the Tower, giving the three women an ethereal appearance. Brishawn stood in the center–tall and pale–flanked by her two sisters, Kishawn and Mishawn, who unlike Brishawn, were wide of hip and bosom.

Kishawn produced a priestly breastplate, inlaid with rare stones, and handed it to Brishawn who draped it over herself. It hung on her pointy shoulders, cumbersome and ridiculous, dwarfing her, and yet somehow she still looked regal.

"We can fix you, baby," she said, holding out her yellow skeleton hand. "Put you back together. But this time we gonna do it with the right parts, hear?"

The Matildas snapped the fingers of their left hands three times in unison.

Worm's mother stood from her wheelchair. They said she would never walk again and yet, she was standing right there, hunched over and unsteady, shaking like a newborn foal.

"How?" Worm asked.

"How, indeed," said Kishawn.

Mishawn pressed her lips together and nodded.

The tall, lithe Matilda produced two mechanisms that resembled nothing Worm had ever seen before. The first seemed to be made from a complex network of gears, levers, and dials, visible through some sort of gold or copper-plated panels. It was long, cylindrical and thicker than the Matilda's forearm.

The second construct's form looked dangerous, as if it were trying to warn you of that danger like the colors and patterns on a poison arrow frog. Brishawn thumbed the switch at the base and the rusted blades that protruded from the end whirred to life. The motor, or whatever device was inside, made a tired buzzing sound.

Worm's mother left with the Matildas that night. He didn't see Nikki again for ten days. The next time he saw her, she appeared shorter. Smaller. And not just because she was hunched over, still shrunken from the fall that had left her mostly crippled.

She had become less than. Reduced.

And yet, she stood on her feet with only the use of a metal drugstore cane.

"They helped me, baby," she said. "Can't you see?"

Worm could barely look at her. "What did they do to you, mama?

"No no, you don't get it. I'm better now, baby. I'm better for you."

"But you're smaller! Something's...different."

"But I'm happy now, baby," she said. "I can walk and I'm finally happy. I ain't sick no more, baby. We're gonna be alright."

Nikki smiled, her gray eyes flickering.

That would be the last time Worm saw his mother.

He needed a weapon and he needed it now. And with him being a felon with no active connections in the streets, there was only one place he could find a gun.

The Matildas.

The night Worm saw his mother for the last time, he watched an unusual vehicle glide down the wrong side of West Fayette Street, other cars honking and yelling at it as it slowly crawled away from the eleven-story brick housing project.

It was a white Delahaye 135M. A car from the distant past that looked like it was from the future. Worm could see everything through the big, fishbowl windows of the historic vehicle, and he swore that what he was seeing was his mother in the backseat, flanked by two brown women, their faces large and moon-shaped. In the front seat was a skinny yellow figure, turned so Worm could not see its face.

His mother turned around so that she was staring directly at him.

Nikki mouthed the words *don't worry* and Worm never saw her again. He knew that it was the Matildas that took her from him. Because he believed the Matildas stole the lifeforce, the essence, of people and places and turned that *élan vital* substance into money or power and then used that money or power to acquire quarter-million-dollar french cars and other things.

Worm didn't really have the mechanics worked out on how they did that, just like he didn't have an explanation for why they lived in Belvedere Towers if they had money, but Baltimore was a weird city and it was what it was.

The Matildas were fucking devils. If anybody knew how to kill a man who thought he was a god, it would be them.

"Turn your brains into soup get your noodle cracked / locked up mixing ramen up with tuna packs / fuck going back to prison I ain't doing that / road to riches you'll think I'm using Google maps"

- Menace Monroe

13

"AGGRESSION COMES FROM ESTROGEN," said the Rebbe, waving his finger in Mordechai's face. "Did you know this? Most people do not. Testosterone is converted into estrogen, you see. This process is called aromatization. When testosterone floods the body, aromatization will attempt to balance out that excess testosterone with higher amounts of estrogen. This process is what causes aggression."

The Rebbe paced in front of the *bimah*. The temperature inside of the synagogue was cool. The pentagon-shaped ceiling's enormous skylights, which began at each corner and ended in the middle, let in light that illuminated the boy's face. Mordechai was thirteen years old, having his Bar Mitzvah less than a few months ago.

The Rebbe, once Rabbi Tzvi, with his degrees in neurology and ophthalmology was a wealth of knowledge and fun facts and trivia.

"The brain is full of many amazing chemicals." The Rebbe motioned for Mordechai to join him in front of the *bimah*. "When I was teaching at CalTech, we discovered where violence lives. There is a region in the brain known as the ventromedial hypothalamus. This is where the neurons for aggression are located. We performed using a technique known as optogenetic stimulation to activate these neurons in the ventromedial hypothalami of mice. We created a so-called molecular syringe out of a disabled virus and used it to inject those neurons with DNA that carried a protein from blue-green algae that increases neuronal activity in response to blue light. We installed mechanisms in the brains of the mice, literal switches that we could turn on or off remotely. Do you understand? We sensitized the violence neurons."

"What was the point of the experiment?" Mordechai asked.

"A good question. We've never had a way to treat pathological violence. Just imprisonment or more violence. We know so little about the basic neurobiology of aggression. A better understanding would be the first step towards better treatment."

"Cool!"

"Yes, cool!" The Rebbe chuckled. "Now let's think about this inversely. What if we want to turn on those special neurons? Nurture the violence?"

Mordechai frowned. "You would turn on the switch, right?"

"Indeed. This would elicit a response in the neuronal activity. With this, you could create an army of perfect little soldiers, ready to do your bidding at the flip of a switch."

Mordechai shook his head. "Why would you want to do that?"

"Why, boychik? With an army of fearless, bloodthirsty soldiers one could accomplish so much. Flip on the switch: problem solved. A perfect arsenal of remote controlled bombs, ready to heal the world through *avodah* and *gemilut chasidim*, no?

"But the Torah forbids us from killing," Mordechai protested.

"Not so," said the Rebbe, waving his finger again. "The Torah prohibits murder. These are different things, killing and murdering."

"How so?"

"Well, killing can be justified in the defense of one's self or another. And in some cases, even in the defense of property. Murder is a different concept entirely."

Mordechai pursed his lips together in a slight frown.

"Killing has a place in Judaism, boychik. An important place."

"It does?"

"Of course. Take our most important prophet, for example. Moses was raised as an Egyptian prince. With that kind of upbringing we can make the assumption that he was skilled in armed and unarmed combat. Probably led a small battalion of soldiers. That is what a prince would do. Moses was not a nebbish or weak man, spending all day and night studying texts. He was the type of man who could lead his people out of slavery. The man for that kind of job would be no push over, I'll tell you that. He was exactly who, and what, he needed to be. And the Egyptian? The overseer who was beating the Hebrew slave? Did Moishe murder him or kill him? What then?"

"He killed him?"

"Correct!" The Rebbe smiled broadly. "Moses was confronted with something he believed was wrong and he did not hesitate to dispatch the wrongdoer. Because, boychik, if you are not willing to commit violence to protect those you profess to love, how much can you truly love them? How much can you truly know love? Does a person like this understand the depths of what love really means?"

Mordechai nodded. "I see."

"But do you? This is very important, Mordechai. The Torah is the story of our people's relationship with *HaShem*, as well as our relationship with our own people. Of course, unjustified killings of our own people is strictly prohibited. But we're allowed to commit violence against other nations in the Torah. Nowhere does it say we cannot kill, raid, and enslave the people of other nations."

Mordechai wasn't sure how to feel or what to say. He felt like he was supposed to say something but didn't know what. But something about the air felt heavy, as if the gravity had changed. Being a Jew meant having a pervasive spirit of doubt and inquisitiveness. With Judaism, the debate was the starting point. It wasn't wrong to question. It was encouraged. He knew he should speak.

And yet he said nothing.

The Rebbe smiled. "Throughout human history, love and violence have always been two sides of the same coin. Men have killed not because they hated the enemy they were killing, but because they loved the people and ideals they were protecting."

"I'm the one who hopped off the porch / fifty pills in my Polo shorts"

- Shy Money

14

Belvedere Towers was a fifteen-minute drive, but Worm didn't have a car. He didn't even have a license. That made the mission a two-hour walk, at least.

Worm watched a rapid transport police van come down Rogers Ave, packed full of QRT officers, masks on faces with rifles propped up against the windows.

The van didn't so much as slow down.

Across the street, two scooters were leaned up against the Magnolia Ave street sign pole. But Worm didn't have a credit card, shit, he still didn't have a phone.

I was more plugged in when I was in prison, he thought, reminiscing on when he was cool with the dude who had multiple cellphones in the dayroom, renting them out until he got caught and put in ad seg, his property confiscated and his canteen privileges taken. Before he was put in ad seg he had shared his phones generously with Worm.

Shit.

He couldn't steal a car. He didn't know how to do that. That wasn't his thing.

Worm heard them before he saw them.

"Stop fuckin playin," he said to no one.

The sound of thin, metallic music gradually increased in volume as they approached.

I was lying on the grass on Sunday morning of last week, indulging in my self-defeat.

They were riding on electric scooters, clad in black gimp suits and matching masks with zipper mouths. Each one with an empty eye socket behind the eye opening. One of them wore a massive bluetooth speaker on its back, LED lights pulsing and changing color in time with the beat of the song.

Worm took in the image of the gimp-suited freaks—riding on rented electric scooters while listening to *Steal My Sunshine*, they were terrifying in their absurdity.

The music was getting louder.

I know, it's up, for me, if you steal my sunshine.

They bent the corner at Rogers Ave, approaching Park Heights Ave in a V formation like migratory birds. The one leading the pack launched itself into the air and came down on top of a man smoking a cigarette in front of a boarded up grocery store. The Antiochian raised both fists in the air and brought them down on the man over and over again, pummeling him while ululating like a Lakota woman. The scooter the Antiochian had been riding flew to the curb and bounced twice before coming to a stop.

The Antiochian with the speaker on its back made tight figure eights in the middle of the street, laughing maniacally, while the remaining two gimps found more civilians to terrorize.

An Antiochian—notably female due to the openings positioned on her gimp suit at the chest and the crotch, exposing her breasts and sex—forehand flicked a serrated chakram at an old man sitting on a bench with the words *Greatest City in America* painted on it. The chakram took the man's head clean off. Black and red viscera sprang out of his neck like jumper cables, his carotid and vertebral arteries severed.

Worm wanted to kill them. He planned to do so when his vision went out. It didn't fade out or blur like before, it didn't even shrink to a pinhole size. It just disappeared completely. He was blind.

The sickness. Was it from the radiation poisoning? An infection from getting bit by one of the Jewish boys? He had been taking his medicine as Dr. Osman had instructed. The pills, the injections.

The Antiochian with the speaker on its back continued to do donuts in the streets while another Antiochian with an oversized machete chased a young drug dealer. It caught up to the drug dealer and plunged the machete into his chest. The Antiochian grabbed the hilt with two hands and kicked the drug dealer so that the blade came out of his chest, pulling out his insides with it. The drug dealer fell to the curb and slumped.

"Making sure I'm not in too deep," sang the Antiochian with the speaker.

And then, like a switch had been flipped, Worm's vision came back. His stomach turned over and he felt a heaviness in his prostate. He tried to slow his breathing, take deeper breaths, hold in the air longer.

An Antiochian at least a foot taller than Worm and twice as wide, got off his scooter and kicked it to the side. The ground seemed to shake when he walked. He ran over to a man selling oils and sacked him like a defensive end.

Worm waited until the sick fuck started pulling down the oil man's cargo pants before he hobbled across the street. He muffled a bloody cough with his fist, then quietly picked up the Antiochian's discarded scooter and took off to Belvedere Towers.

"And I always got a lot on my mind, that's why I be pacing"

- YNE Sosa

15

THE REBBE WAS BORN Amram Menachem Tzvi in a basement in Pimlico, the child of Holocaust survivors. There was never a time when the Shoah wasn't part of his consciousness. A constant spark in the back of his mind that reminded him that no matter how great his suffering, it would be shameful to complain, because his hurt could never amount to the pain that his parents endured.

His father would go to the *mikvah* then come back and say, "You know that the Shoah was our punishment, yes?"

The Rebbe got up from the lounge chair and sidled up to Mordechai. He placed his hand on the boy's shoulder and continued. "Mordechai. Do you understand the difference between a rabbi and a Rebbe?"

Mordechai shook his head.

"Both come from the Hebrew *rav,* but this is not what is critical. You see, a rabbi answers questions, whereas a Rebbe answers people. A rabbi hears what you say with your mouth. A Rebbe hears what you are saying with your soul. Does this make sense, Mordechai? Are you following me?"

Mordechai nodded. "Yes, I think so."

"I can hear your soul, Mordechai. I'm working every day to make *Olam HaBa* happen, this is our mission as Jews. Build heaven on earth, as it were."

"What is the difference between *Olam HaBa* and *T'hiyat HaMe-tim*?" asked Mordechai.

The Rebbe scratched his eyebrow. "*Olam HaBa* is The World to Come, the afterlife, whatever that may be. *T'hiyat HaMetim* is the resurrection of the dead, a specific occurrence that isn't necessarily directly connected with the former. But as most things are with our people, it is a *machlokes* of terms. Maimonides says not to worry about these things. They will be what they will be. There is not enough information in the *Tanakh* or *Chazal* to be definitive. In Judaism, there is a constellation of concepts that deal with the end times. But there is no agreement on the exact meaning of these concepts, the order in which they will occur or how long they last. Will the resurrection of the dead occur during the messianic period or after it? Does *Olam HaBa* exist for the departed immediately after they die, or is it something that occurs in the future, after the messianic era is over? Or both?"

"I see."

"I like to believe it occurs during the messianic period. The resurrection of the dead. This sounds so pleasant, no? *T'hiyat HaMetim?*"

Mordechai said nothing.

"Mordechai, are you aware of who I am?" the Rebbe asked. "Do you know me?"

Mordechai furrowed his brow.

"The job of *HaMoshiach* is to bring all the Jews to Israel, yes. But technically this is the second stage. First *HaMoshiach* must get all Jews to become fully observant, and he has to fight the wars of God. We are here to fight the wars of *HaShem*. Do you hear this, Mordechai? To fight the wars of God?"

Mordechai licked his lips. "Yes. I hear what the Rebbe is saying."

"I feel it coming, told my brothers we don't have long"

- JackBoi Dummy

16

Toomp CAME TO AND spit out the tip of his tongue. Tasted wet nickels. His head swam until he remembered the girl. Vision sharpened.

"Stupid bitch," he said, tasting fresh blood.

This was not good. Not at all. The tips of tongues didn't grow back. A panic set inside of his chest, deep and burrowing. He would need the tip of his tongue at some point. He felt like he needed it right then and the whole *not having it* part made it that much worse.

That stupid bitch.

He had only wanted to speak to her, say hello. Yeah, he had his dick out. So what? She didn't have to do all that. Damn near tased him to death.

Toomp crawled into the Malibu and collapsed in the driver's seat. He slumped over the steering wheel and shook off a few more electric seizure wiggles. What was left of his tongue felt fat and heavy.

"Oh, you stupid bitch," he said again, pounding his fist on the dash. "Oh, how I hate you so."

All of his *S's* sounded like *Th's*.

That's what a tongue detipping will get ya, he thought.

He sounded ridiculous when he spoke now and he knew it. Like one of those homosexuals. Toomp didn't have a problem with homosexuals, not one bit. He firmly believed that a man's dick was for providence, fucking anything and everything, human, animal, alive and occasionally dead. Gender and labels were for stupid motherfuckers who couldn't get in touch with their true self. No, Toomp didn't have any problems with homosexuals.

But he didn't want to sound like one.

He needed to get back to his office. Needed to get somewhere safe and get some shit inside him. Something to blur the edges a little. Then, when things weren't so sharp, he could formulate a plan.

He reached under the passenger seat for the *jile*. It was heavy in his hands as always. The rhinoceros horn handle was cold, like holding a bag of ice. He ran his fingertips along the truncated brass fixed on the pommel. The sheath was made of wood wrapped in white leather, skin stained brown with dried blood from regular use, and the tip of the sheath terminated in a large brass orb adorned with ornate filigree.

He drew the dagger from its sheath and felt its weight in his fist. Its coldness. His fingers wrapping around the smooth bone. The sharply curving fifteen-inch fullered blade, widest at its center and constructed from salvaged metal plates, recovered from broken leaf spring suspensions found in truck wreckages. The blade was double-edged and looked like a long, asymmetrical leaf. Impossible to find outside the Horn of Africa.

The Afar—the people of the Danakil Desert—were known to castrate and murder intruders with the *jile*. And all the men carried them—strapped to their waists, the scabbards attached to leather belts with circular buckles. It was said that an Afar man could only marry *after* he had cut off an adversary's testicles.

Toomp fantasized about cutting off a faceless stranger's testicles. He would use his left hand to wrench their penis up to their stomach and his right to swing the *jile* underhanded and clip the ball sack off in one fluid motion. Would it work? Or would he have to lift the ball sack up? Really pull on it and stretch out the scrotum so he could saw it until it was nothing but thin skin and connective tissue?

Then he thought about cutting off his own testicles and stuffing them down the throat of the woman who tasered and beat him. He thought about her choking on them, how they would fill up her mouth. Really push her cheeks out like a chipmunk, make her look so ridiculous, while he bled from his taint to his boots. He thought about his boots filling with his own blood until his feet sloshed inside them and the strange gagging, duck-like noises she would make as he pinched her nose closed. Push it all in there. Slap his hand over her mouth. Ball sack asphyxiation death. His amputated nuts in her throat, drowning her.

The thought of it made the blood rush to his dick. He cried out in pain. She had injured him pretty badly. There was something wrong with him, and not just his missing tongue tip. She had got him good. One too many times in the bean bag, maybe. Getting hard hurt now. That would go away eventually though, right?

It would, right?

Toomp relaxed as his erection dissipated, the pain washing away with it. The curved blade of the *jile* glinted in the windshield, casting a long shadow across the Malibu's dash. The *jile* was more than a weapon, more than just a tool—it was a connection to Djibouti, a link to the people he had touched and tasted and pushed and pulled during his time there. He felt their legacies through the bone handle.

He scanned the parking lot, every nerve in his body sparking like jumper cable clamps on battery terminals. He needed to head back to the Mount Hope-Seton office on the other side of the Plaza. There was paperwork to do. Forms to complete. Some email from HR about open enrollment and how he needed to pick a new insurance plan since the city had awarded the contract to a new insurance company.

Something about switching them to United Healthcare and how he had to pick between the gold plan or the silver plan or the bronze plan. He would have to find all new doctors and dentists and that would be an inconvenience.

There were multiple pending DPSCS investigations against him. But he didn't care about that. Technically, he should have been removed from the field and put on admin duty the moment he had even one grievance filed against him, and not because they were worried about his conduct but because of the state's fear of lawsuits. His caseload should have been split up between multiple agents in the area. But the system was convoluted and it was hard to find people who wanted to work for DPSCS. They were horribly overworked and understaffed.

He needed to show face, too. In general. Make the rounds. Let people ask him how his weekend was so they could go off about whatever stupid-ass shit they did with their stupid-ass weekend. It was important to be present.

And the 2F-ketamine had worn off while he was unconscious.

He would have to do something about that.

"Listen, I was the one in the trenches / scraping the hard on the dishes"

- Bandhunta Izzy

17

WORM HATED THE MATILDAS.

Hated everything they stood for.

So it came as no surprise that in order to save the Westside, he would need their help. It was just the kind of day he was having. He put the kickstand down and left the Antiochian's scooter on Falls Road.

The Westside Matildas represented everything that was wrong. Wrong with Baltimore, the future, progress, life, however you wanted to look at it. At least that's how Worm saw it. They didn't make sense. Their whole existence.

His fierce hatred came from his lack of understanding of them, of what they were. But really, did he even have to try? They were Matildas. They didn't deserve understanding. They didn't belong in the city and he didn't *want* to understand them. He just had to tolerate them, and only until he got what he wanted from them.

Worm felt his blood pressure rising the moment he saw the plastic folding chair levitating in front of Belvedere Towers. The chair hung upside down in the air, bobbing up and down like a fishing float.

"Fucking Matildas, yo," Worm muttered under his breath. "The worst!"

But he came here for a reason. For a weapon that had been rumored to kill gods.

Worm didn't know any gods, but he knew men who believed they were gods. Men who used every resource at their disposal to manipulate and control others. Men who preyed on the weak and easily influenced the feeble-minded.

Worm went inside the lobby and took the elevator to the 12th floor. He walked down the hall, the muffled thump of club music bass coming from one of the apartments, shaking the walls of the building. The door opened before he could knock. A small child with floor-length hair, their gender impossible to determine, beckoned for Worm to come inside the low-rise unit.

Two of the three Matildas—Kishawn and Mishawn— sat on a faded blue futon, one knitting a length of yarn into a scarf or blanket, the other with her eyes shut and hands clasped together tightly in her lap. They were both large women, wide of hip with massive bosoms, thighs that touched whether they sat down or stood. Their skin glowed golden-brown like warm chestnuts, their smiles a permanent fixture on their round faces. The third Matilda, Brishawn—tall and pale—stood lithely in the kitchen by the clouded window above the counter and turned the pages of a cookbook without using her hands. Worm watched her flick her wrist in the air, the pages turning with each delicate movement. She looked fragile standing in the same room as Kishawn and Mishawn.

God I hate these Matildas, Worm thought, but said nothing. He tried to make his face unreadable. No sense offending these witches and having to leave without getting what he came for.

Worm cleared his throat. "So, look right, I know y'all don't fuck with me like that but—"

"Say less," said Brishawn, without looking away from her cookbook. "We know why you're here."

"Yes!" said Kishawn said, waving her finger at Worm. "We know!"

Mishawn's laughter was musical. "Why you're here, yes. Indeed, we do!"

Worm frowned. "Oh ard. That's what's up then. So you know what I need, right?"

Brishawn waved her hand, abruptly closing the cookbook. "Yes, yes. You wish to kill a god. I said *say less,* did I not?"

"A god?" yelped Kishawn.

Mishawn laughed again. "He wishes to kill a god?"

"Well, not an actual god." Worm tucked a loose dread behind his right ear. "Just a regular ass dude who thinks he's a god. Or maybe not even a god, for real. More like the assistant to a god or some shit like that. Whatever a messiah is."

Brishawn walked over to Worm and took his hands in hers. "Does he have followers who think he's a god?"

"Well, I mean, yeah, I assume so. I figure he has a few folks behind him. That's how this shit usually works, right? A motherfucker say he the next Jesus or messiah or whatever the fuck, and some folks believe him. Gets himself a little army of dumb motherfuckers who wanna be a part of something so bad that they compromise what little integrity they have to believe his bullshit. That army becomes his congregation and all that. You know how it go. Like some Waco or Jim Jones shit. Except this motherfucker a Jew."

Brishawn let go of Worm's hands and turned away. "So, you say this man, who has followers that worship him like a god, but is not a god, requires a god-killing weapon to defeat him? Are you retarded?"

Worm sucked his teeth. "The fuck? Why I gotta be all that?"

"Retarded!" squawked Kishawn.

"He must be," teased Mishawn, a sing-songy lilt in her voice.

"Hey, look here," Worm said, turning towards the two Matildas sitting on the futon. "Y'all just keep repeating the same shit shorty say, like y'all her whole hypeman team or some shit. With ya cheerleading asses. Ain't got a thing in the world to contribute to the conversation. Adlibbing and hyping. That's all y'all do. But y'all calling me retarded. Shit."

"Mind yourself," said Brishawn. The frail Matilda twisted her wrist and made a fist. Instantly, Worm felt his testicals flatten against his thigh, then rise higher as if they were trying to go back inside him. "Now, apologize to my sisters."

Worm bit down on his tongue to keep from losing consciousness. "OK, OK. My bad y'all. Shit! I'm sorry. I ain't mean y'all no disrespect. Come on, yo!"

Brishawn squinted at him. "What happened to your eye?"

"Dumb shit," Worm hissed through his teeth. "Greeks, you know how they be doing. Come on, yo, please!"

Worm felt the pressure release as his balls fell back into place.

"Remember," said Brishawn, "this is our domain. I implore you to behave while you are here."

Worm caught the copper taste of blood in his mouth. "This shit is a three-bedroom unit in a high rise. This shit ain't no *domain*. I hear you, though."

"And yet, here you are." Brishawn smiled and held her hand out, palm side up. "In our home asking us to help you kill a man who thinks he is a god."

Mishawn raised her left hip off the couch and farted.

Kishawn covered her mouth and giggled.

"I hate y'all so much," said Worm.

Brishawn sighed. "Will the things you have shared with the world so that the world will believe you have value, these nonsense things you have done with your life—will these *things* be what saves you in the end?"

Worm felt a cold emptiness in his lower intestines. The androgynous child appeared again with a plate full of something dark green and puréed, spinach or collard greens, perhaps. White cubes—tofu or cheese—floated in the leafy mush.

The child held the plate in front of Worm. "Palak paneer?"

"The fuck?"

The child smiled at him. "Would you like some palak paneer?"

Worm felt a wave of nausea and realized it was almost time for his dexamethasone injections. "No," he said. "I'm good, yo."

The child turned and disappeared down the hallway that led to the Matildas' bedrooms.

Brishawn was staring at Worm. "You may have noticed that many of the city's streetlights have turned purple."

"No." Worm touched his empty eye socket. "I was only out of prison for a day. Then I was in the hospital right after. I ain't seen shit."

"The lights of the city have begun to turn purple."

"OK."

"Some people compare it to a dark purple, or like a black light. BGE says that the reason for the change in the color of the streetlights is that they didn't properly anticipate the conditions these lights would need to endure, that these early model LED lights couldn't handle being subjected to so much thermal cycling stress at high temperatures. They tell you that it causes the bond between the phosphors and the LED chip to become damaged. Tell you that this causes a large drop in the yellow light generated by the phosphor, so the blue light from the LED coming through without any conversion gives the streetlights that purplish glow."

Worm swallowed. "What the fuck."

"It's a lie," said Brishawn. "The reason I know this to be a lie is because *we* did this. My sisters and I have turned the streetlights of Baltimore purple. Some of them, anyway."

"They tell lies!" the Matildas on the couch yelled. "Lies!"

Worm was about to tell the Matildas that that was the stupidest shit he had ever heard when the androgynous child entered the room once more, their hair sweeping the ground like the leaves of a weeping willow. They held a guitar case wider than they were, and longer than they were tall. The child set the case down and unlocked it. "Can I open it?" they asked.

"You may," said Brishawn.

Kishawn and Mishawn slid closer to one another on the futon and wrapped their arms around each other. They hugged each other close and pressed their swollen bellies together. "Open it!" they cried out in unison, their voices melding together and humming like a sine wave.

The child opened the case and Worm was underwhelmed. "God-damnit," he said, pinching the bridge of his nose.

Inside the case was a 24kt gold-plated Thompson submachine gun. Bright as the sun. Sparkling in the poorly lit project house. A street sweeper from the Roaring Twenties, clandestine, archaic and dipped in a meretricious expression of opulence. The stupidest shit ever.

Useless.

"This bitch is supposed to be a god-killer?"

Brishawn slithered over to Worm and stuck one, long, spiny finger in his chest. "And you're supposed to be a hero, no?"

The two Matildas sitting on the couch said, "Awwwwwww," their eyes full of laughter, like two children in school, mocking another child for getting in trouble; two large children with floor-length gray dreadlocks making the same childish sound as an elementary school classroom.

Worm shrugged. "So, what does this thing do anyway?

Brishawn put the kettle on without touching the stove. "Your *god-killer* is what we call the William Donald Schaefer. It doesn't shoot regular bullets. The drum creates its own ammunition. It pulls the opiates out of the Baltimore air and converts the poison into projectiles. These projectiles are little exploding missiles of carfentanil. This is one hundred times more potent than fentanyl. Do you understand?"

"No," said Worm. "That's some wild ass shit to say to a person. The fuck you mean do I understand?"

The tall, pale Matilda scratched her elbow and frowned. "I don't know why the city chose you. You think this is funny. "

"No, I–"

"Maybe not *funny*," Brishawn cut him off, "but you think because *you* don't care what happens to you that what happens to you won't affect others. But it will. You don't think I remember you? You think I don't remember your mother?"

"Don't ever talk about my mother."

Worm could only harbor so much hatred for the Matildas for what they did to his mother. In the end, it had been her choice to leave. No one had forced her to get inside that white Delahaye. And he never truly knew what happened to her. Just that she had left by her own volition. But he wasn't going to let them speak about her. That was for sure.

"Clearly, you aren't built for any of this. But for some reason, you're the one. I hate to say it, but it's true. You're in all my visions. You always have been."

Worm clapped his hands together and stepped backwards. Then forwards. He cupped his hands around his mouth and yelled to no one in particular. "Oh shit! Now she got visions. I'm 'the one,' ok.

You on your *Matrix* shit. That's what's up. When you start having visions, huh? Y'all Matildas not like that, for real. Y'all just out here in the Towers, moving shit with your mind or magic or money or all of the above. Whatever the fuck y'all on. Now you got *visions* and shit. Leave me out your visions, yo."

Brishawn touched her middle finger to her thumb and closed the guitar case. The Matilda beamed at Worm, a tear forming in the corner of her eye. "Save the Westside, save the world."

Worm took the William Donald Schaefer and left the Towers.

"I seen my lor mans lose control / he caught a body he was seventeen and that was twenty years ago"

\- GGL Slick

18

"The streetlights, Mordechai," said the Rebbe. "You've seen them, have you not?"

Mordechai nodded.

The Rebbe sneered. "Hate them, I do. I hate them so very much."

Mordechai thought the occasional purple streetlight was quite pleasant, like the silent glow of heat lightning on a summer night, devoid of thunder or rain. Just a warm flash of something calming and beautiful as you passed by.

"The state is always cheaping out on our city," the Rebbe continued. "Cutting costs, the *schmucks*. They do this up and down the avenue, they do. At the light in front of the Seven Mile Market. On Reisterstown Road. The one at Labyrinth, also. They cheap out on components instead of getting the right lights with high quality diodes like they do in the county, and Howard and Montgomery, the *schmucks*."

This was why they had the *Hatzalah*, the northwestern Jewish community's response to the mismanaged and underfunded emergency medical services provided by the city. *Hatzalah* was volunteer-based, with a team of over forty certified first responders, twenty dispatchers and seven state-of-the-art transportation units.

If you couldn't trust the *goys* with the infrastructure then you definitely couldn't trust the *goys* with your life, obviously. It would be naive to think otherwise. And that was the reason for *Hatzalah*. That was the reason for many things. But it wasn't like there was a problem with not being a Jew. Jews didn't proselytize. People could do as they wished.

Something had been troubling Mordechai. The Rebbe's experiments, his chemicals, all of it in the name of gathering Jews across the city and *encouraging* them to become more observant. After the city, the counties would be next. And what then? Bring all of the Jews back to Israel like the Rambam instructed? It wasn't realistic. It was completely out of order. *HaMoshiach* would come after these things had transpired.

Everything was out of order.

Everything was wrong. Mordechai felt a sweat droplet run from the base of his neck down the center of his back, squirming along his spine like a worm on a fishhook as it went down.

"Mordechai?" the Rebbe asked. He was staring at the boy, the edges of his eyes curled up in annoyance. "Are you paying attention? The streetlights. The situation is absolutely dreadful. You don't see those hideous purple lights in Annapolis or Ellicott City. Terrible."

Mordechai nodded and hugged his velvet *tefillin* bags.

"He locked up and ain't coming home / so it's Green Dots and Obama Phones"

- Tate Kobang

19

THE ANTIOCHIANS PATTED EACH other on the back and slapped fives. They regarded their masked faces, slick with blood, one with a tooth embedded in the leather that covered the forehead area.

"Hey, Tyrell!" yelled an Antiochian named Van Cleef. He wielded a bloodstained machete. "You got somebody's tooth stuck in your fuckin head! Ha!"

The one with the tooth in his head, Tyrell, plucked the ivory incisor from his mask and ate it. Then smiled.

"This guy!" said Van Cleef.

The Antiochian with the speaker on his back continued to do figure eights and donuts in the middle of the street.

Van Cleef pointed at him. "Hold up, hold up. You see this fuck? Get the fuck off the scooter, Pontoon. You fucking clown. You been scootin and scootin your bitch-ass around this whole time. I didn't see you do shit! Your mask is still clean, you fucking dumped out sewing needle kit."

Pontoon stopped circling, his mouth zipper turned down in a frown. "Dumped out sewing needle kit?"

"Yeah, I said it. Nothing but random thread, a caved in thimble and buttons that don't go to anything. That's what you are, Pontoon. A dumped out sewing needle kit."

Pontoon hopped off his scooter and kicked it to the side. He skipped over to Van Cleef, removed the speaker from his back and smashed it over the other Antiochian's head. Sparks flew and the music slowed to a melting stop.

If you steal myyyyy sunnnn...

The Antiochian dropped the machete and fell to his knees.

"Pontoon, you dickhead," Tyrell chided. "Now we don't have any tunes."

Black blood ran out of the Antiochian's mouth hole, the speaker on his head concealing the upper half of his mask. His left leg jerked a few times then settled.

Pontoon slumped. "He insulted me."

"So what?" Tyrell waved a finger at him. "Words are just words."

"But they were hurtful. They were hurtful words."

Tyrell opened his zipper mouth and put a wine Black and Mild between his lips. Torched the end of it. Puffed it a few times to get it lit. "Next time, I implore you to think first before acting on your impulses. We must try to be practical. We must not waste our violence."

"You're right. Perhaps my behavior was too rashly."

"Goddamnit, Pontoon."

"What did I say?" he asked, tilting his head.

Tyrell sighed. "The word you were looking for was *rash*."

Pontoon narrowed his eye. "I don't have a rash. Don't start telling people I have a rash. People already say disrespectful things about my hygiene practices, because I prefer to use a loofah instead of a washcloth, but I tell people this, Tyrell, I tell them that I just really like how my skin feels much cleaner after I use a loofah because–"

Tyrell shook his fist. "Oh, you! No one cares about your stupid loofahs or your–"

"Look at Fontal and Sloan!" screamed Pontoon, cutting off Tyrell. He pointed towards a transformer box where Fontal, an obscenely obese Antiochian, had the female Antiochian, Sloan, bent over the green box, eating her from behind. "Look at them go!"

Sloan's tits hung out of two circular openings cut into the gimp suit. They swayed back and forth as she pressed her ass into Fontal's face. The fat Antiochian's tongue hung out of the zippered mouth, lapping at a third hole, cut into the crotch of Sloan's gimp suit.

Tyrell palmed his forehead. "This is ridiculous."

Pontoon skipped over to the copulating Antiochians and tried to get one of Sloan's nipples in his mouth.

Fontal wasn't having it.

The giant Antiochian bear hugged Pontoon to his chest, lifting him off his feet. "I'm not in the mood for your shit today, Pontoon. I'll crack your fucking chest open!"

Sloan stood up and laughed at the scene. "Crack his fucking chest open, Fontal!"

Fontal squeezed Pontoon a moment longer, then dropped him to the ground. "Not worth it."

A woman's corpse lay half off the curb, her faux locs falling into the street. Blood ran from the top of her head and down into the sewer drain.

Tyrell rang the bell on his scooter. "If you three are done playing grab-ass, get your scooters and let's keep it moving."

Pontoon retrieved his scooter from where he had tossed it aside before killing Van Cleef. Sloan picked up hers, then zipped up the breast and crotch openings in her gimp suit.

"Hey," said Fontal. "Where's mine?"

The Antiochians turned left and right.

"Over there?" Sloan pointed to the scooter that lay next to the dead Van Cleef, with the speaker still sticking out of his head.

"Nope, that was Van Cleef's," said Pontoon. "He dropped his scooter and machete when I was addressing his disrespect issues."

"You didn't *address his disrespect issues*," Tyrell said. "You smashed a speaker over his head and killed him in the street like a civilian."

"OK, fine. When I smashed a speaker over his head."

"And?"

Pontoon slumped. "When I killed him in the street like a civilian."

"Let's move on then?" Sloan was growing impatient. "We know that *that* scooter," she pointed, "was Van Cleef's. And Van Cleef is dead, so now we have an extra scooter. Just take his scooter, Fontal. He won't be needing it anymore, am I right?"

Sloan nudged Fontal in the side, but he wasn't interested. "No," he said. "I don't want Van Cleef's scooter. I want *my* scooter. The scooter I was riding is gone. And *that* scooter is connected to the app on *my* cell phone which charges *my* bank account! I need to find that scooter."

"So just end the ride on the app!"

Fontal couldn't find his phone. "It must have fallen out somewhere," he said, patting the pockets on his gimp suit.

"Goddamnit!" shouted Tyrell. "You don't even need your phone. I'll log in to your account on my phone and cancel it for you."

Pontoon sniffled. "But don't you think it's weird that a whole scooter is missing? How does that happen?"

"He's got a point, Tyrell," said Sloan.

Fontal fumed. "Who gives a fuck about the scooter? I need to find my phone and cancel the ride so I don't get charged."

"But we need to know who took it, right?" asked Pontoon.

"Fontal," said Tyrell. "If you give me your goddamn account information I can get on my phone, cancel the ride so you won't get charged, and also see where the scooter is."

"Or *is going*," said Pontoon.

"What does that mean?" Tyrell asked.

"Well, if it's gone, maybe somebody is riding on it right now."

Tyrell considered this. The idiot had a point. "Fontal? Your account information, if you will."

Fontal waddled over to Tyrell while Pontoon attempted to get a hand on Sloan's crotch zipper. She slapped his hand away and shushed him. Fontal gave Tyrell his login and password for the rideshare app.

The two Antiochians huddled around the phone, while Tyrell swiped and tapped on the screen.

"What's taking so long?" asked Fontal.

Tyrell huffed. "It's...just...really difficult to see the screen with these fucking masks."

"And the whole only-having-one-eye-thing makes it even more difficult, am I right?" said Sloan.

"You ain't lying," Tyrell said. "Those Greeks really fucked us up."

Sloan shrugged. "Better than being afraid all the time."

"I, myself, have never been afraid of anything," Pontoon said, hands on hips with his chest puffed out like a rooster.

"Shut up, Pontoon!" the other three Antiochians yelled in unison.

"I can't see shit with this goddamn mask," hissed Tyrell. The Antiochian pulled the mask up so that it sat on his head. One of his eyes was missing—which was normal for Antiochians—but there was an angry, red line of infection that ran from the empty socket, over his jaw line and down his neck. Tyrell sighed in relief. "So much better."

Sloan, Fontal and Pontoon stared at the infected wound. "You should probably get that checked out," said Sloan, pointing at Tyrell's face.

"Checked out? Are you retarded?"

"Don't call her that," growled Fontal. He grabbed Tyrell by a steel ring hanging from the center of his gimp suit and pulled him close. Lowered his voice. "And you're not supposed to say *that* word."

Tyrell drew a neon pink XVR 460 S&W Magnum from his utility belt and thrust it up under Fontal's throat. "Don't you be prudishly passive aggressive with me, fat man."

"Wait!"

Pontoon was pointing at the phone held precariously in Tyrell's hand. He had almost dropped it when he upped the revolver on Fontal. "Take it," said Tyrell, giving the phone to Pontoon while still holding the gun to Fontal's throat, while Fontal still kept a vice grip on Tyrell's chest ring with his silverback gorilla strength.

Pontoon swiped and tapped. "Let's see here."

"You have no idea what you're doing," groaned Sloan.

Tyrell cocked his head at Fontal. "Are we done here?"

Fontal let go of Tyrell's chest ring and lowered him to the ground. "Indeed. I grow weary of this."

Tyrell put the revolver back on his hip.

"I found it!" Pontoon was hopping from foot to foot. "I found it!"

"Hand it here." Fontal grabbed the phone out of Pontoon's hand. "The scooter is moving. It's moving down the Avenue. It looks, it looks like it's near Druid Park Drive. Or maybe the zoo or something. Or maybe Reisterstown Road. I don't know. These fucking masks, man! It's so hard to ever know what's going on."

Tyrell snatched the phone from Fontal. "Give me my shit. Let's follow this fuck."

The Antiochians hopped on their scooters and rode down the street, ululating and swerving into traffic while Tyrell pointed his sex-toy-pink revolver at civilians.

"Standing on the corner like a crossing guard directing shit / telling all the junkies wait five minutes then come in a split"

- Lor Scoota

20

WORM WAS CRUISING DOWN Falls Road, one hand steering the Antiochian's scooter with the other hand holding the guitar case, when the machine gun spoke.

"Nobody understands showmanship anymore!" the gold gun yelled, its voice that of an old white man with a strong Baltimore accent, muffled inside the guitar case and fired up as all hell. "When I was mayor of this city, I painted the curbs of the city pink. The Harbor? Ha! Nobody even wanted to go there. It was a no man's land. The harbor was just a place for dumping the bodies! I gave the people *real* street theater. And yeah, so what, I called the reporters *little girls,* but back then, the reporters were all men, so it wasn't disrespectful to women, you understand? I was calling men *little girls* to disparage them. Not the women, because there were none. They were sensitive little fucks and I called 'em like I seen 'em. *Esquire* called me America's Best Mayor. This city has gone to shit."

Worm squeezed the brakes on the scooter and brought it to a stop. He put the case down. Bent at the waist. Put his hands on his knees. Hung his head so that his dreads touched the ground. "Come on, yo."

"When I was mayor, I was all about making it happen. I don't see you making it happen, you mook. I made Oriole Stadium happen. Fucking Camden Yards. That's my legacy. What's your legacy?"

A stud with wide hips and a septum piercing walked up to one of the low-rises and fumbled with her keys.

Worm stood up straight. "You hearing this?"

The woman opened the door and rushed in, reminding him that he had an exposed, empty eye socket.

"I lived on Edmonson the whole time I was mayor," the gun said. "That was my mother's house. You understand me, you mook? The whole time."

"Yo!" snapped Worm. "I don't care about none of that shit. Stop talking, yo. Please. Just please stop talking."

"Who do you think you're talking to, tough guy?" the gun snapped back. "I know you're not talking to me! This fuck can't be talking to me. I was the mayor of Charm City! That's not a job for the faint of heart. I bet you couldn't do it."

"And I don't want to! I never said I did."

"You're a mook," the gun said from inside the guitar case. "That's what I know."

Worm tried to get back on the scooter but his knees gave out. His sphincter tightened and sheets of cold sweat formed on his cheeks and forehead. His surroundings blurred into smudges and smears as if he were looking through a filthy window. His veins pumped ice water. His spine was made of toothpicks. His vision narrowed further as if the world was closing in on him, colors bleeding together and turning to mush. Sparks of light danced in the corners of his mind. Black tadpole-shaped things swam around his head. He gripped the handle of the scooter tight, determined not to fall.

An old woman coming out of her building stopped to look at Worm. "People like you are the problem," she said, adjusting her church hat.

Worm choked. A muffled thumping voice. Someone was speaking to him. "What?"

"Young man, I won't deny the impact of the murders and violent crime here. You can't get no new residents and investment money in the city until you make a significant reduction in crime. Look at the bid to get Amazon. They ain't want nothing to do with us! The city was offering up an insane package and still wasn't picked. Why? Because of the crime, sure. But nah, it ain't just the crime."

Worm felt like he was underwater.

"Harbor East," the old woman continued, "and all the recent development in the city happened when the murder rate was down. That's what you gon' say."

The sun burned into Worm's forehead and he vomited on the sidewalk, splashing the scooter with it.

The woman shook her head. "Disgusting! But it's not just the murders. It's about taking care of these babies. The poverty that feeds this dirty city is driven by generations of children with parents who don't give a damn what they do or don't do. They not learning no appropriate or goal-driven behavior. These innocent babies grow up in survival mode and become teenagers, too fast for they own good, and then they go off and create new generations of children who will be raised by grandparents who can't retire, or parents that's locked up, addicted, or dead. That's how you end up in survival mode. How you gonna contribute to the betterment of your community when you just trying not to die in it? That's you, young man. You did it. You killing the babies. But you just a lost baby too. I know.".

Worm tried to speak but only a hiss came out

"What's that, young man?"

"I'm trying," he said. "I'm gonna shoot at the right thing."

The woman studied Worm disapprovingly. "Grown man tryna ride a scooter, can't even ride a scooter. You don't need to be shooting at anything."

"Growing up my brother always told me cash rules / like a cell facing the wall I had bad views"

- Soduh

21

Toomp was watching scat porn on his laptop at the Mount Hope-Seton office when he got the call from the house operator at St. Ambrose who informed him that his new client, Worm, had neglected to show up for orientation.

Toomp was not sure how angry he wanted to be about this. Anger felt good. Anger was a natural drug that you could keep injecting into the center of your brain by thinking about more things to upset yourself and then your anger grows and evolves and you start feeling it in your teeth, like an icy mouth guard, and then you just...purge. You purge and release. Release and purge. The process of purging warmed the teeth in the most pleasant of ways. Like sinking a bite into a warm croissant. Oh, how he loved it so. Toomp loved drugs, especially the natural ones.

Anger could be represented visually by the performance of a neuron dying under an electron microscope. In the footage Toomp had seen, the neuron looked like pizza, stretched taut at certain points, relaxed at others, the surface of it smooth like warm cheese. The neuron looked like the skin of a starfish, pulled in asymmetrical directions. When the neuron died, the stretched points retracted back into the core. The neuron went completely white, but in a way where it was nothing and also everything.

Anger felt like that *looked*. Like a neuron dying. Like all of the neurons dying and being reborn, stretching out and snapping back.

But anger also took a lot of energy, and Toomp was exhausted from his marathon 2F-ketamine jerk-off session in the parking lot behind Douglass High School.

Technically, he had still won that game.

And there was his afternoon visit with Randy. That little rendezvous had taken a toll on him as well.

Nothing tested his patience more than dealing with Polacks. Toomp hated the white trash Polish that populated the southern corner of East Baltimore. Hated their stupid last names with all the consonants in the wrong places, combinations of hard sounding letters, grouped together in ways that didn't make sense. How was anyone supposed to know that the letters *Z* and *E* made a *CH* sound. And they were always the first motherfuckers to stumble over the pronunciation of a Nigerian or Ghanaian last name. As if those surnames weren't all vowels, arranged in patterns that make sense, pronounced exactly how they looked.

Toomp hated not knowing things immediately. Hated to be corrected by anyone.

And then there was the woman who had destroyed his genitals. The reason that he was watching scat porn in an objective way, a way that was only tangentially related to the concept of arousal and climax.

Because it hurt too much to think about it.

But he would keep hope alive. He would try it out every so often, see if his shit worked. Keep trying. Never give up. Fight the good fight.

"I'm incredibly disappointed to hear that," he told the house operator. "I had high hopes for this one, but then again, I have high hopes for all my boys. I'll take care of it."

Toomp ended the call and put his phone down. He unpaused the scat porn and watched a woman shit in another woman's mouth. "You dirty whore," he said, taking his hand out of his pants. He closed the laptop and got up from his desk. Fired up a Cadillac. Sucked the filter end, exhaled blue smoke into his meticulously organized office.

Toomp remembered his time in South Africa spent tracking down weapons dealers. The campaign covered the worst kind of terrain. Having to share water with the locals because they never remembered to bring their own. It never made sense to Toomp, which made him think the locals did not deserve to live. Because they gambled on their survival. As if their lives were fleeting stones rather than precious ones, meant to be cherished and protected.

Fuck those stones.

They knew they needed the water. And if they knew they needed water to live, why did they never have any water with them on the hunts?

This is why Oloman Toomp believed they had no right to be alive. None of them.

If they didn't care enough about their own lives to water them, why should he care? And why should *he* be the one to water them, to tend to their gardens? Or anyone, for that matter. Everyone's lifespan was nothing more than a culmination of all their decisions, and some people made some dumbass decisions.

Stupidity was when you didn't know what to do. That's it and that's all. It's a special kind of hybrid ignorance mixed with arrogance when you knew what to do and *still* didn't do it.

Toomp took another pull from the Cadillac. The cherry glowed in the dimly lit office, creating a small oasis of orange light around his mouth.

Life's a journey, and for some folks, it's meant to be a short one, he thought to himself.

They tracked the warlords through the brush for fifteen miles, stepping on branches that occasionally turned out to be venomous snakes, doing their best to avoid running into crocodiles. The dealers started fires. The dry shrubland burned, turning it into an inferno.

Toomp recalled running through the fire to reach the dealers on the other side, the flames singeing his hair and turning his eyelashes white.

Toomp recalled the way the Rigby .416–a weapon designed for hunting elephants and other big game–opened up the first dealer's chest and left an exit wound in his back the size of a medium pizza. How the opening in the man's chest looked like a portal to another world. Like a dying neuron, stretching, pulling. Swirling reds, fuschia and burgundy. He remembered sticking his finger into the wound, scraping the edges of it. The heat of the wound. How steam rose off it and how everything smelled like iron and shit. How the iron and shit smell seemed to coat his nostril hairs and stay there for days after.

He felt himself getting hard–or he thought he did–but his dick remained flaccid, draped over his left thigh like a dead Mexican mole lizard. He was aroused–the scat flicks and anger had made sure of that–but nothing was happening. He felt the blood rush from his loins but nothing moved. That bitch did a number on his manhood.

But he still had his arms, his legs, his fists. He still had his tools. And he still had the *jile*.

The *jile*.

Tucked away, hiding. Contained. The *jile* hated being alone.

He would have to do something about that.

"White people walk up on me, askin' why my pants low"

- A$AP Ant

22

"Wait!" screamed Pontoon.

The Antiochians pumped the hand brakes on their scooters and huddled in the middle of Northern Parkway. Cars swerved to avoid the black mass of gimp-suited freaks. A Ford Fiesta came too close. Tyrell pointed his pink gun without looking and fired three times. Two of the bullets went through the back windshield of the vehicle, causing it to hop up onto the sidewalk and plow through a bus stop.

Tyrell replaced the gun and put his hands on his hips. "Now what could be so important, Pontoon?"

"I just," Pontoon began, "I just think that there's this huge misconception about us. That because we like to hurt people and kill people, that we don't eat. Not that we don't like to eat certain foods. But that we don't eat, period. Like, at all. As if murder negates the need for sustenance. But fuck sustenance. What about my desire to eat *good* food? Not just food for food's sake."

Tyrell got off his scooter and put the kickstand on. "Goddamnit, Pontoon. Get to the point."

"OK. I will. But remember, it's faster to make dinner without adding seasoning, but what kind of life would that be?"

Fontal rubbed his belly. "No life at all. That's for sure."

"Not you too," groaned Tyrell. More cars swerved and Tyrell emptied the revolver cylinder. He reached under the leather at his ankle for a fresh moon clip, found one, slapped it in the dog.

"I'm just saying." Fontal shrugged sheepishly. "He's got a point."

"He's trying to make an excuse for talking in circles. He does this. You have to understand. That's his *thing*."

Pontoon slumped. "That's not my *thing*, Tyrell. People don't think that's my thing. Do they?"

"No," said Fontal. "They don't think that."

"I do," said Sloan.

Pontoon looked like he had been slapped. "What?"

"It's definitely your thing," Sloan said. "You always do this shit. Just get to the fucking point, man."

Pontoon hesitated, tried to find his words. "Well, like I was saying. I think people should know that we enjoy food and eating and other pursuits, beyond just murder and mayhem. And that we are cultured in that respect. Like me, for instance, I really like the yat gaw mein at Pimlico Carryout. I like Hey Daddy's. I like that they can make you a cheesesteak with shrimp on it, which is great for someone like me, because I can never decide between shrimp and steak, and Hey Daddy's puts me in a position where I don't have to. They set me up for success because I don't have to choose. Does that make sense?"

"Are you high?" asked Tyrell.

"Well, yeah," said Pontoon, scratching his head. "Of course. Isn't everybody?"

"I'm not," said Fontal, folding his arms and raising his chin proudly. "I never use drugs. I'm all about fitness and treating my body like a temple."

Pontoon looked the other Antiochian up and down. "What are you talking about? You're fat as fuck!"

The corpulent Antiochian got off his scooter. "Take it back!"

"Fine," Pontoon acquiesced, making himself smaller. "I shouldn't have body-shamed you. I apologize. I'm aware the data suggests weight stigma is more pervasive than racism, and even sexism."

"Thank you." Fontal backed off. "You know, weight discrimination is a big part of the obesity problem, not the solution. If fat-shaming worked there would be no fat people. I implore you to consider that."

"I miss Van Cleef," Pontoon said.

"You killed Van Cleef!" shouted Tyrell.

"I know, but still."

"Still what?"

"Just still. I miss him. That's all."

"You're an idiot."

Sloan shook her head. "You really are an idiot."

"You're not supposed to body-shame!" Pontoon pointed his finger at Sloan and Tyrell. "Stop body-shaming me."

Sloan facepalmed. "That's not what body-shaming is."

"My brain is in my body." Pontoon grinned, stretching out his mask. "You were shaming my brain."

"He's not going to get it," said Tyrell.

"So back to what I was saying." Pontoon was on his scooter, circling as he spoke. "I think it's a misconception a lot of people have. Like, because they think we're monsters, that means we don't eat? That we don't like to eat? I'm just saying it's a misconception."

"I think it's like how you never see somebody take a shit in a movie, or read about them taking a shit in a book," Fontal offered. "It doesn't mean the writer thinks people don't shit, that the characters don't shit. It's just not necessary. It has no relevance to the message the artist is trying to convey. We eat food, yeah, some of us even like it. But we also murder people in the pursuit of glorious art and that kinda supersedes everything else. That's a much bigger part of our branding."

Pontoon scratched his chin. "I guess that makes sense. I think I'm just really hungry. We could get food right now and change the whole narrative."

"Shit!" said Tyrell. "Fontal. Check your phone."

Fontal's one eye widened. "Fuck," he gasped, pulling out his phone.

The stolen scooter was going west on Northern Parkway, back towards Park Heights Avenue. The Antiochians fussed with each other a bit more, then hopped back on their scooters, riding and screaming at the sun as they chased the stolen scooter back to the Heights.

"If you ever been to Baltimore people get killed for nothing"

\- BRM Stuntin

23

Worm got off the scooter and kicked it into the street in front of the Ellenbergen Center. He hoisted the guitar case up. The sidewalk gutters were clean, free of refuse and broken glass. The property of the religious facility was well maintained. Jew Town was so different from the rest of the Heights.

The William Donald Schaefer squawked from inside the case. "Look, buddy. I'm no antisemite. I helped Robert Weinberg launch the Jewish Museum of Maryland. People tried to tell Robby, they tried to tell him, shit, nothing good can come from building something down that way. Lloyd Street was fucked up back then. I mean, it's fucked up now, but it was especially fucked up back then, you understand? But I gave him the money. I put the money in the project because I believed in him and it turned out to be a great success and I'm no goddamn antisemite! You have to understand this."

"What's your point?" asked Worm, hating himself for talking to a gun.

"Something don't seem right here."

Worm tore the wrapper off an alcohol pad and swabbed his upper arm. With steady hands, he unwrapped a new syringe and popped a fresh needle out of its packaging. He drew the dexamethasone up into the syringe, then tapped it lightly, watching the air bubbles rise to the surface then disappear. He positioned the needle against his upper arm at a 90-degree angle and pushed it into his skin. There was a sharp sting, followed by a sensation of immediate relief. For a moment his skin felt normal, no longer feeling like he was being burned alive. He pressed the plunger down until the syringe was empty then withdrew the needle. His skin began to tingle at the injection site.

"Good grief," groaned the machine gun. "This mook is a junkie. We're fucked!"

"It's medicine for radiation poisoning," Worm replied.

"Then we are really fucked!"

The doors to the Ellenbergen Center swung open. Two men in long, black coats poured out, their faces sharp and angular with chiseled jawlines and baseball mitt hands that one-fisted heavy, iron pernachs, as thick as telephone poles, with menacing flanges on the mace heads like arrow fletchings. They were tall with broad shoulders and long twisted *payot* that bounced as they approached, forced to hunch over in order to make it under the doorframe.

"Shit," Worm said, tossing the needle. He set the case on the sidewalk and opened it. The contents reflected the sun and momentarily blinded him. He took the golden machine gun and lifted it up. Steadied it. It was lighter than it should have been. As if it were hollow.

"What I tell you?" said the gun. "I knew something was up. I told you I ain't no goddamn antisemite. Well, what are you waiting for, you mook? Charge me up."

Worm upped the William Donald Schaefer at the men and pulled the trigger. The golden gun began to vibrate. Worm felt the sensation go from his hands around the grip of the gun to the molars in the back of his mouth.

"Fuck yes!" the gun screamed. "I'm the fucking mayor!"

A series of red LEDs began to rapidly light up around the drum. The lights turned green and stopped moving and the drum itself began to spin. There was a whirring noise that increased in pitch as the spinning of the drum magazine intensified. The men were within an inch of being able to take the stupid gold gun off Worm's stupid ass and beat him to death with it when the drum stopped spinning and the machine gun made a ding noise, like the sound of an egg timer going off, and the carfentanil rounds deployed. Three holes opened up in the first man's neck and he fell to the ground.

"Damn," Worm said. "I thought you were gon shoot darts or needles or something."

"Are you touched?" The machine gun was panting. "Your elevator don't go to the top floor, or something? All the buttons are working but the electricity is out? Why would you think that?"

The other man raised the pernach above his head and swung it down at Worm. He tried to sidestep but couldn't get out of the way fast enough. The mace glanced off his shoulder and cracked his humerus. The pain exploded in his arm and shot up behind his eyelids. The injured arm fell to his side, limp and useless. His good arm still held the machine gun.

The Hasidic man lifted the pernach above his head once more, readying himself for the final death blow, when the Antiochians showed up.

"You might hear my phone ring in my songs cause sales be calling / I'm deep in that water, my wrist flooded like New Orleans"

- Roddy Rackzz

24

"THERE HE IS!" THE four Antiochians arrived on their scooters and fanned out in front of the Ellenbergen Center. Pontoon pointed an accusatory finger at Worm. "Thief!" he screamed. "You dirty, no good thief! Shame on you!"

The Hasidic man held the pernach in the air as if frozen in time. Worm cowered under the cartoonishly large mace with his one good arm above his head to guard himself from the oncoming blow. Nobody moved.

"Shit," Worm said.

"Shit is right." Fontal was speaking now—much larger than the other three, much more imposing, the gimp suit barely containing his rolls of fat. The zippers and black leather looked ready to pop. He cracked his knuckles. "You took something of mine, and I intend to get it back."

"Well, technically it isn't *yours*," said Pontoon. "You were utilizing it, yes, but you were simply renting the scooter. You don't own the scooter. As far as property laws go and all that."

Fontal facepalmed. "Goddamnit, Pontoon. This is not the time for semantics."

"Just playing Devil's advocate." Pontoon winked.

Fontal shook his head. "I won't entertain that. I refuse to. Devil's advocate is a narcissist's game and I won't play it with you. Play with yourself."

"You told him to play with himself!" Sloan leaned against her scooter, some of her long, auburn hair sneaked under the neck opening of her gimp mask and spilled out over her shoulders. She made a jacking-off gesture and laughed loudly.

"Enough!" yelled the Antiochian who hadn't spoken yet. Tyrell. An oversized, neon pink revolver on his waist and some kind of oversized cleaver on his back, like something a giant would use to cut up giant cow meat. "I've had enough of this shit. No more."

He stepped off the scooter and shot the Hasidic man in the face with the neon pink XVR 460. The pernach clattered to the ground with a metallic thud, bouncing once, then coming to rest on the sidewalk where the flanges caught the light of the sun and looked like shark fins. The man dropped to his knees. A crescent-shaped chunk of his skull was gone, as if a shark had taken a bite out of the top of his head. Instead of tipping over, the Hasidic man stayed on his knees and died with his shoulders slumped forward.

Two more men, as big as the first two, burst through the doors of the Ellenbergen Center. The clothes they wore were the same but they had removed their long, black cloaks, exposing their starched, white button-up shirts. One held an oversized pernach like the other two before him. The other man one-fisted a piece of rebar, one end sharp and jagged as if he had torn a piece of structural work off a building in the process of being built.

Sloan kicked her scooter aside and took the chakram off her back. The polished surface of the weapon shimmered, making it look like she was holding a miniature sun.

Tyrell aimed the revolver at Worm and pulled the trigger. Worm winced. The gun dry fired. "Fuck!" the Antiochian screamed. He tossed aside the empty weapon and snapped his fingers.

Fontal reached for the handles of his Ka-Bar knives, which were strapped to his utility belt. His swollen, sausage-fingered hands moved like a symphony conductor, pulling the blades out of their sheaths with fluid, practiced grace.

Pontoon picked up his scooter and flipped it upside down, holding it like a club. "We could really use some theme music right now," he said.

The high-carbon steel of Fontal's blades, polished to a mirror-like sheen, caught the light of the sun. He gritted his teeth. "You're the one who fucked up our speaker."

Worm slipped inside the Ellenbergen Center as the Antiochians and Hasidic security team collided.

"I'm whippin work, Howie, Goodie / Slick Al caught a body in a black hoodie"

- Caddy Da Don

25

THE RESURRECTION OF THE dead was a core belief in the *Mishna* and the Rebbe was no charlatan. He embodied the thirteen foundations of Judaism. His way of thinking aligned with Nachmanides' definition of perfection, living by the adage, 'the higher something is, the lower it can fall.'

To imagine that the body was just a mere vessel, temporal and destined to be reduced to dust. This was the way most theological thinking went. To consider the corporeal form too imperfect, too temporary a place for the perfection of God to exist, was an insult to God. To think that God only dealt in the spiritual was to relegate God to *some* things rather than *all* things, which would be just as troubling as attributing physical properties to him. The Rebbe knew that God was capable of both spiritual and physical things because God created all things spiritual and physical.

The World to Come would not be a spiritual world of disembodied souls, but a world in which spirit and substance expressed the perfection of their Creator. According to the Rebbe, the resurrection of the dead would lead to eternal physical life.

T'hiyat HaMetim.

Rabbi Amram Menachem Tzvi would make this happen, for he was *HaMoshiach* and this was his calling. An army of the undead. Jewish undead. His army.

Worm walked into the sparsely furnished lobby. Wooden benches lined the walls. The sun had moved across the sky and amber light filtered through the angled glass panels of the atrium ceiling, diffusing it and bathing the room in a soft, radiant glow. A few simple sconces hung unlit. There were no paintings or photographs or framed certificates. No ornaments or curios. The walls were devoid of adornment of any kind beyond the tarnished, silver sconces.

Worm put the machine gun under his arm and massaged his injured shoulder. He took a few more steps forward.

The lobby of the Ellenbergen Center spoke to the humility of Chassidic tradition, reminding visitors of the importance of modesty. The bare walls. The austere oak benches. Worm took a closer look at the walls. As his eyes adjusted to the lighting, he noticed that the gray paint was not uniform, but instead, there were patches of darker and lighter shades that created an unsettling, mottled effect. As if it had been painted and then painted over, again and again. The color seemed to shift and change depending on the angle of his gaze, as if the walls of the building were alive, responding to his presence.

He looked harder.

The texture of the paint was also off. He could see that now. Rough and uneven, with cracks and bubbles that seemed to writhe and twist like grotesque organisms. It was as if the paint were trying to break free from the walls, to escape its confines and infect the rest of the room with its asymmetry.

At the opposite end of the lobby was a door to another room. A small mat lay on top of the polished concrete near the entrance.

Worm opened the door.

The Rebbe sat in the octagon shaped room, the walls and floor as black as oil. The man was a striking figure; his muscular build obvious in the way his broad shoulders and bulky arms filled out his black suit. His hair was jet black under his kippah, his mustache neatly trimmed—his beard long and streaked with gray. Dark, green, piercing eyes picked Worm apart from underneath thick, expressive eyebrows.

Mordechai stood next to the Rebbe, feeling small. The ceiling glowed with some kind of LED overhead lighting that pulsed and swelled.

"You think you're God or some shit?" asked Worm. The William Donald Schaefer hung at his side, silent for once. "That's what this is?"

The Rebbe smiled. "A part of God, yes, but it is more complex than that. There is no clear place where the Rebbe ends and God begins."

"Right, like I said."

"God chose to imbue this world with life through a body."

The Rebbe nodded at Mordechai who walked across the room to a control panel mounted on the wall and flipped two breakers. Worm tightened his grip on the machine gun.

"The Rebbe is the conjunction of God and human," the Rebbe continued. "The Rebbe is God, but he is also physical."

"All this shit sound dumb as hell. You know that right?"

The Rebbe patted his thighs. "Yiddish is an extremely dynamic language when it comes to insults. We have three different words for *loser*. Did you know this?"

"Here we go."

"One of my favorite explanations of the three Yiddish terms for *loser* comes from a great man, a man by the name of Arnold Fein. You see, there can be *schlemiels*, *schlimazels*, and *schmendricks*, and they're all different. Let's say the *schlemiel*, *schlimazel*, and *schmendrick* were all sitting at the dinner table. Well, you see, what will happen is the *schlemiel* will spill his wine all over the *schlimazel* and the *schmendrick* will apologize and make a mess trying to clean it up. You see?"

"Right. Which one am I?"

The Rebbe winced. "No, no, no. You are a *schmuck*. This is different."

Worm laughed and swung the William Donald Schaefer up so that it was aimed at the Rebbe. "Tell me why I shouldn't kill you now?"

"Because you're curious. You still want to know my purpose. You want to know yours. You want to see this through, no?"

"I wanna know why I just had to fight a pack of murderous Jewish children in a 7-Eleven. Why the fuck their jaws open like that?"

"Ah yes," said the Rebbe. "My little army. What happened with my little soldiers was simply a miscalculation. My figures were off. I'm not immune to failure, you know."

"Shoot this crazy fuck already, will you?" the William Donald Schaefer squawked, breaking its silence.

Worm said nothing.

"Put the talking weapon down," the Rebbe said. "Let me show you something."

"Do it! Do it!" the William Donald Schaefer was chanting. "Take his fucking head off!"

"Fuck it." Worm pulled the trigger and held it.

The William Donald Schaefer wheezed. The drum did not move. Nothing happened.

The Rebbe rolled his eyes. "Your ignorance is why you thought that would work here."

Worm pulled the trigger again and again. "The fuck?"

The machine gun hacked and coughed. "Something's wrong. It hurts. I'm not working. I'm not working. Help me, Jesus. Oh God!"

"Heroin is for the blacks and the South Baltimore whites," the Rebbe said. "You're too far up the Avenue for that, *boychik*. As I have said, your weapon will not work here."

Worm let the machine gun fall to his side. "Well, fuck you too then, you mook!" it barked from his hip.

"Please," the Rebbe beckoned. "I have something I must share with you."

And then the Rebbe told a story.

"I'mma catch him and peel him / swear to God I'mma kill him"

- Lil Cuz

26

TOOMP JUMPED THE CURB and slammed the Malibu onto the sidewalk, landing the nose of the car inches away from a bleeding Antiochian's head. The song in the car was "Rush"byPaula Abduluntil he hit the press-to-start button and pulled the fob out. Paula stopped crooning about how she was gonna take this love right to ya and the probation officer got out of the car—tall, upper body defined, big arms, with a disgusting, distended, bowling ball belly. The muscles were a testament to discipline, time in the gym spent honing his physique. But the swollen orb attached to his midsection represented discipline deferred; indulgence embraced.

If Toomp was anything, he was an indulgent motherfucker.

Toomp put the vape pen to his lips and pulled, sucking his cheeks in, making himself look older. The cathinone passed through his blood-brain barrier with a lightning snap to his nervous system. He counted to ten then exhaled, blue vapors fogging his Costa Del Mar sunglasses.

Toomp whistled and took the Costas off. He looked down at the gimp-suited freak and sucked his teeth. One of its eyes was missing. Just an empty, blackened hole. He nudged it with the toe of his boot, then kicked it when it didn't move.

Toomp had never seen anything like it.

And he couldn't give a fuck less that he hadn't.

Whatever this thing was, the ridiculous aesthetic, the blood on its hands and torso, the dried blood on its mask and knees; all of that indicated that it was a monster of some kind. As pathetic as it was. Otherwise it wouldn't go outside in Baltimore looking like that.

"I don't know what the fuck you is," he said, stepping on top of the dying Antiochian, "but one thing for certain, two things for sure, somebody rocked you boaaaa!"

Toomp crouched down on top of the Antiochian's chest and grabbed the zipper on its mask. He pulled the metal tab across its face and held his hand an inch from its mouth, checking to see if it was still alive. Labored breath like butterfly wings against the palm of his hand.

"I feel you breathing, bitch."

He didn't understand the appeal of the gimp costume and S&M buffoonery. Couldn't tell if it was male or female, black or white. Its skin looked gray, almost. A dark off-white, camel hide, newspaper-that's-been-sitting-in-the-rain-for-days kind of color.

Toomp stuck a dirty finger into the Antiochian's mouth, twisting it around and scraping the inside of its cheek. He pushed the finger in further until the Antiochian's back spasmed, throwing it up in an arch and knocking Toomp back. It vomited all over itself, then propped itself up on its elbows and panted like a dog. Toomp stood up, then got back down on top of the Antiochian.

The two monsters stared at each other.

Toomp took out the *jile* and plunged it two-handed into the Antiochian's mouth. Black blood sprayed over his wrists and forearms.

"I don't give a fuck what you are, ya overstand me?" Toomp said softly, twisting his grip so that his palm was on the butt of the rhinoceros horn handle. The Antiochian's leg twitched. "I don't wanna know your story or why you out here dressed like a dyke bitch's strap-on. I don't give a fuck about none of that. I done killed all kinds of shit. Whatever you is, I done killed so much worse and none of it, knamean, none of it come and kill me yet."

Toomp put his left hand over his right and dropped his weight into the brass pommel of the *jile,* burying it to the hilt. The tip of the dagger struck concrete. Toomp twisted his body to the right and the Antiochian's head came apart, the black gimp mask holding on for dear life to keep the sections of face and skull together in their original form.

The probation officer wrenched the *jile* out of the Antiochian's mouth, the sound of it like pulling a shovel out of wet sand. Wiped it off on his chest. "See, the thing is, the thing is I'm the baddest motherfucker out here. I'm the paragon of physical prowess, you dig? The baddest thing walking. I say *thing* because I know there's more than just men out there. I know cause I've met em. And they done met *me*. I ain't never had to stare into the abyss to get like this. I *am* the abyss. Believe that! So I don't give a fuck about none of what you got going on. I'm here for one thing, and one thing only, and that's to collect my property and lock his bitch-ass back up, feel me? And that's exactly what I'm gon do."

Toomp stood up from the dead Antiochian and started towards the Ellenbergen Center.

"I got the yat gaw mein, beef and that broccoli, serve you an eggroll you can't get the sauce"

- Skeeno

27

TYRELL STOOD OUTSIDE THE Ellenbergen Center and watched a man he had never seen before murder Pontoon.

That was interesting.

Part of him felt bad for Pontoon. Unlike Fontal and Sloan, Pontoon had been an idiot, destined to die sooner or later. Fontal and Sloan were warriors. Their deaths were warriors' deaths.

Antiochians' deaths.

Pontoon was ignorant in a cute and innocent sort of way. Like a spider that eats all of its babies because it is hungrier than it is smart. Pontoon was *that* kind of cute and Tyrell felt sorry for the poor little spider.

The man pulled the curved blade out of Pontoon's mouth and stood up. Tyrell bit the leather of his mask.

The man started to walk towards him.

Fuck it, I'm from Antioch, Tyrell thought, then took the weapon—which was more than half the length of his body—off his back and pointed it at the man. "Who the fuck are you?"

The man stopped a few feet away. Put his hands on his knees and leaned forward, bending at his knees and nearly squatting, then standing up and leaning back. "Nigga, is that from *Bloodborne*?"

Tyrell inhaled sharply. "No."

"Yeah yeah, nah, nigga, nah. I don't know about all that. Lie to your daddy, don't lie to me. That shit you got there is from the video game *Bloodborne*."

"Is not!"

"I don't know why you so worked up about it," said the man, pointing the curved dagger with the white horn handle at the Antiochian. "If you like it, I love it."

Tyrell studied the three-foot long cleaver at the end of his weapon. The blade curled inward, back towards the handle, exposing a serrated edge outwards. The other side of the cleaver, blocked by the handle, was smooth. Soiled bandages were wrapped around the length of the blade. "It's custom made. I had it made just for me. By a professional metallurgist."

"Nigga, what?"

Tyrell frowned. "A metallurgist. A person who works with metal. Like a blacksmith, if you will."

"A welder?"

"Kinda. Yeah. Like a welder, I guess."

"Why you ain't just say that then?"

"What?"

The man laughed. "Why you ain't just say a welder made that goofy-ass bullshit for you? That's what I'm asking you. Hold up. Chill. I'mma answer that question. I know why you ain't say that shit. You thought *welder* sounded too ordinary. You was, like, thinking people wasn't gon take you seriously enough. You was all like, 'I bet if I use a cool word like *metallurgist*, motherfuckers will be impressed.' That's what you thought, huh? You ain't gotta say shit. I know the answer already."

Tyrell pouted under his mask. "You don't know what you're talking about."

The man stood up and pointed the dagger at the oversized cleaver weapon. "I ain't even gon hold you, that shit look like you got it off *Etsy*."

"What?"

"*Etsy*, nigga! Shit."

"We'll see about that," said the Antiochian, swinging the weapon in an arc from his upper left shoulder to lower right hip, causing the three foot cleaver to unhinge and snap out straight, nearly doubling the weapon in length.

The man stepped forward and grinned. "Let's go then."

Tyrell swung the gargantuan weapon with fervor, aiming to end the fight in a single blow, but the other man was too nimble. He sidestepped, no, teleported almost, and the cleaver whistled through the air, missing the man entirely and continuing its downward trajectory until it slammed into the concrete. The impact sent shockwaves through the handle and up the arms of the Antiochian, causing his grip on the weapon to falter. Tyrell could feel the vibrations electrocute his teeth.

The probation officer took advantage of this and closed in on him, grabbing one of the steel rings on his gimp suit and plunging the *jile* into the soft part between his ribs. The man twisted the blade so that it was angled vertically, and then drove it upwards. Deeper. Tyrell vomited blood and the man ripped the knife out of him, pulling out dark red tentacles of viscera. The cleaver fell to the ground.

Tyrell watched the long ropey things tumble out of the hole in his body. "But wait," he sputtered.

"What's that now?" Toomp held the tip of the blade to Tyrell's remaining eye.

"I knew it," the Antiochian gasped, peppering Toomp's face with black blood. "I knew it from the moment I laid eye on you."

"Knew what, fuck nigga?"

"That you were a warrior. Like me. That's how you knew my weapon was from *Bloodborne*. Games like *Call of Duty* and *NBA 2K* don't do it for men like you and I. Art and entertainment exist in the same sphere, but whereas the former has complex intent, requires audience interaction, involvement, participation, all that, the latter is simple garbage, spoon-fed to an audience of idiots. Every day, every waking moment of our miserable existence we're inundated with waste, like shit-flavored infant formula sprayed down our throats through feeding tubes. Rarely art. Never art! I got an endoscopy once and that's what it feels like. Like being throat-fucked by nonsense. Everything we come into contact with is focused on making money, and by extension is almost exclusively entertainment. *Bloodborne* is different. *Bloodborne* manages to balance the line between these two ideologies beautifully. Art and entertainment. There is complex intent, there is enjoyment, but it's not handed to you. The true beauty of the game is that the *real* fun, the *real* story, requires the player to actively seek it, which provides a feeling of joy far grander than what you might find playing the latest *Call of Duty* or *NBA 2K.*"

Toomp stared at the Antiochian, blinked once when a piece of his small intestine hit the sidewalk with a smack.

"Like I said." Toomp launched a barrage of quick strikes with the *jile*. "Etsy."

Tyrell was caught off guard, unable to defend himself from the onslaught while the man's *jile* found its mark time and time again, piercing flesh and cutting through shiny black leather. The leaking Antiochian, the life pouring out of his body with each strike, stumbled backwards, then crumpled wetly onto the sidewalk like a discarded marionette.

"You getting alotta action today, babygirl," said Toomp to the *jile*, wiping off both sides of the blade on his black t-shirt and returning the dagger to the small of his back.

Toomp snorted back phlegm and other evils and hocked a cluster of gray mucus the size of a small organism on the sidewalk. He stepped over the bodies, Antiochians and Chassidim, and went inside the Ellenbergen Center.

"Long as I got a plug and some baking soda no need for friends"

- YGG Tay

28

"LONG AGO, IN THE city of Prague," the Rebbe began, "our people were under threat. We were persecuted. Violated. Brutalized. Our people were filled with fear, for they knew that they were outnumbered and vulnerable."

Mordechai punched a code into the keypad mounted on the wall then stepped back. Worm saw the faint outline of a towering door appear in the reinforced steel wall.

"The Rabbi of Prague, a wise and learned man known as the Maharal, sought to find a way to protect his people. He retreated into his study and pored over ancient texts, seeking guidance and inspiration. He called upon his knowledge of the Kabbalah and crafted a Golem out of clay. He breathed life into the Golem, and with the secret combination of letters passed down orally from master to disciple, he placed the *Shem* in its mouth and imbued it with incredible power."

A faint humming sound filled the air, growing louder and more intense by the second. And then, with a sudden jolt, the door began to move. Massive steel plates ground against each other, sending a shower of sparks flying. Mordechai shielded his eyes. With a thunderous clank, the door lifted.

At first, all Worm could see was a dark silhouette. It was a looming shadow that seemed to fill up the entire space inside the wall. Worm stared into the black, letting his eyes adjust. The outline took on a three-dimensional form, a hulking mass of earth and stone, roughly sculpted into the shape of a man. It was asymmetrical—the right arm twice the length and thickness of the left. Intricate patterns and otherworldly symbols were etched into the creature's stony skin.

Something about it was off. More than just the asymmetry of its form. As if it had been sculpted by a creature that only knew what a human looked like from hearing one described by something else that wasn't human either.

Its face was featureless, devoid of any openings, mouth or nostrils, save for the two hollowed out craters that served as its eye sockets.

Inscribed on the forehead were three Hebrew letters.

"*Emet*," said the Rebbe. "It means *truth*."

Worm stared at the massive statue– its skin cracked like the floor of a dried-up lake.

"At first, the Golem obeyed the Maharal and guarded the Jewish community with fierce loyalty. The Jews of Prague were grateful for the Golem's protection. However, as time went on, the Golem's power grew too great. It became uncontrollable, killing any and all non-Jews, not just those that intended to do us harm, for it perceived all *goyim* as a threat to our people. So it went on a rampage, and it killed and maimed and burned and bludgeoned anyone who wasn't Jewish. Desperate to restore order, the Maharal found a way to remove the *Shem* from the Golem's mouth and deactivate it, which he did."

Mordechai wiped his brow with the back of his hand. It felt like the room was getting warmer.

"Now here is the part where retelling of the story differs," the Rebbe said, holding his hands out. "Some suggest that the Maharal destroyed the Golem, while others claim that it was hidden away in the basement of the synagogue and has remained there for centuries."

"Not gon lie," Worm said. "That's a good story."

"Ah. Yes. Perhaps it is just a story. Perhaps it is just a cautionary tale about the dangers of creating something that is beyond our control."

"OK."

"But it is not just a story. It is not just a metaphor. It is our history. It was a solution to a problem, a problem solved by a great man. But even in his infinite wisdom, the Maharal made a mistake. You see, the Golem had not become corrupted. The Maharal had not lost control of it. The Maharal created the Golem to protect the Jewish people from all threats, and anyone who is not Jewish *is* a threat to our people. *All* threats. Always. It has always been this way. Throughout history we have been enslaved and hunted and tortured and experimented on and *othered* by every host nation we reside in. They call us inferior while simultaneously claiming we control the entire planet. That we are a lesser race. It is incumbent upon us to understand our greatness and believe in it so that we do not cheapen and profane ourselves. The Golem was simply working as intended. Better than intended, if you ask me."

The Rebbe produced a tiny piece of parchment and placed it to his lips. He spoke into the scroll, his hands cupped around his mouth, muffling his words.

The Rebbe removed the parchment from his lips. "I will not make the same mistake," he said, placing the *Shem* in one of the Golem's eye caverns.

"Pick em up, pick em up"

– Griff and Booman

29

WHEN IT TOOK ITS first mouthless breath of life, it felt a sharpness. This sharpness crawled through every inch of what it had begun to understand as its being. When it experienced—but never physically saw the dim lighting of the penetralium, because it had no eyes to open— it felt pain for the first time. As it experienced this pain behind the front part of its face, the sharpness traveled down into its extremities.

It had fingers and its fingers were big and thick and made of familiar rocks and clusters of masonry. These chips and chunks and fragments of masonry were from somewhere of importance, somewhere holy, a building perhaps. A temple.

Its body was formed of earth. From the rocks and earth of Prague. Prague. Which meant something. Sandstone and shale and particles of organic matter.

It was bedrock.

It was sand and silt and clay.

It felt as if it were made of plaster. Thick slabs of papier-mâché, slapped on top of the rock and earth and whatever it was made of underneath that. Wrapped around a wire skeleton like bandages until it became what it was.

It looked upon the Rebbe first and what it saw was all light and the light was good. It looked upon the *goy* nextand knew pain for a second time. It knew fear. It felt as if it were made of dead things and things that had never been alive, and so it was in fact made of death, but only at that moment did it come to know this to be true.

It was death given life. And what was that? That made no sense. No sense at all.

The sharpness came back and shot through the Golem's skull, then bounced around inside of it like .22 caliber bullets ricocheting inside of a person's guts. It raised its arms—one much bigger than the other—then pounded its chest like a silverback gorilla. It rushed Worm and slammed itself face first into the wall when he slipped out of the way. A crack ran through the wall where the Golem's head had connected with stone. Plaster crumbled and fell from the ceiling.

The Golem slapped itself in the forehead like it had been stung. It had no mouth and could not scream. It had no eyes. Just those expressionless, cavernous sockets in its pie-shaped face. But it flailed about, continuing to slap itself in the forehead as if that would accomplish something.

"Now, I told you," snapped the William Donald Schaefer, "I ain't no antisemite. But this is some—"

The Golem reached for the talking machine gun and flung it across the room where it hit the wall and exploded into what looked like thousands of golden LEGO bricks.

"Look at that!" the Rebbe cried.

At that moment Mordechai realized everything was completely fucked.

"All my Glocks got a drum or extension / push the button it start up the engine"

\- CTM Ball

30

Toomp high-stepped into the penetralium and saw Worm first. He didn't see much else after that. Maybe in his peripherals he might have seen some dumb shit.

He was always seeing dumb shit in his peripherals.

Maybe he saw a Jewish man with a beard in all black and the boy in similar attire by his side. Maybe he saw a giant monster made of clay and stone.

And he couldn't give a fuck less if he had.

This was because a man's peripherals were for the dumb shit. A man had to stay focused. Eyes on the prize type of mentality.

He was here for one thing and one thing only.

"Alright now," he said, gesturing with the bloody *jile* for Worm to follow him. "I ain't gon fuss or fight with you. Eyes to the floor or I'll split you from appetite to asshole, and you know it. Gotta get your bitch-ass downtown and I ain't getting stuck in no rush hour. Come on then."

The probation officer was drenched in blood from his shiny forehead to the tips of his boots. His shirt had a burn mark on it— a circular untouched hole in the center of his chest surrounded by a ring of charred, blonde, discolored material, almost like the black shirt had been bleached. Like a glazed donut. The front of his jeans were dark with blood, both new and old. Caked with dried semen. It looked like he had gotten busy before getting his dick shot off.

It was kind of like he had. Gotten his dick shot off, that is. Just as bad. Couldn't get hard no more anyway.

"Oh shit!" yelled Worm.

The Golem punched a hole in Oloman Toomp's chest, right in the donut-shaped burn mark. The back of the monster's fist came out the back of Oloman Toomp, pushing some of his insides out with it. The Golem twisted its fist and then opened its hand, upturned, palm facing the sky, fingers curled as if beckoning. Then it pulled its arm back out through the probation officer's chest; its thick clay fingers wrapped around lumps of dripping entrails.

Toomp's jaw dropped. Blood leaked out of both corners of his mouth in identical crimson rivulets, trickling down his jawline and running down his neck. He tasted the metallic tang of it mixed with the cathinone drip in the back of his throat.

The last thing Oloman Toomp saw was the autostereogram of his *own* soul. This was an autostereogram Toomp had always wondered about. Didn't know if he had one. Until now. And it was glorious.

It was a grid of dots. A series of spirals. A collage of geometric shapes and fractals, overlapping images and intricate patterns, in every color in the spectrum and some colors that he had never seen before and had no names for.

The patterns of pixels were aspects of his life, his memories, his experiences, all woven together into a complex and intricate tapestry of him and all that he had been.

He let his eyes go unfocused and saw the hidden image of the autostereogram—the face of his father.

The old man's face was weathered and worn, like a piece of driftwood that had been battered by the waves and tossed upon the shore.

His mouth, a thin line set in a permanent frown; his lips dried and cracked. A scraggly beard flecked with gray. Deep-set, weary eyes. Eyes that had seen too much of the world and found it wanting. Eyes that flickered with a strange light that seemed to come from some far-off place, like the last ember of a dying fire.

His autostereogram father lit an autostereogram Cadillac and Oloman Toomp died on the floor of the penetralium.

"You'll see so many drums you'll think a parade coming"

– Tyree Colion

31

AMIDST ALL THE INSANITY, Worm had gotten behind the Golem. Using his good arm, he reached up and around, and with the monster's body blocking his line of sight, he blindly searched its eye sockets. The Golem raised its big arm above its head. Worm found the *shem*. He pulled it out and the Golem powered off like a desktop computer.

"Oh shit! It worked! I wasn't sure that shit would work, but that shit really worked!"

The Rebbe rolled his eyes. "Mordechai? Will you please dispatch him? We have pressing matters to attend to."

But Mordechai had gotten behind the Rebbe while Worm was getting behind the Golem, and at some point he had taken the *jile* off Oloman Toomp's body. He ran the *jile* across the Rebbe's neck and a thin brushstroke of blood followed behind the blade.

Mordechai cut the Rebbe's throat.

He dropped the *jile* to the ground where it clattered amongst the golden pieces of the William Donald Schaefer.

"Goddamn," said Worm. "Why you do that?"

"He was sick," Mordechai said. "I had to do something. What do you mean?"

"Yeah, I mean, obviously. But I thought you were with the shits."

"I'm with Judiasm. I'm a Jew. I'm not with whatever this is. What it has become. He was a good man. But he was sick."

"Yeah, OK."

"You shouldn't judge others until you've stood in their place."

Worm's bad arm had completely lost feeling. This was curious to him, and not just because the otherworldly pain was gone, but because the lack of feeling had made him begin to feel something close to fear. Fear that he might lose his arm like he had lost his eye and his amygdala. Fear that he would lose more parts of himself.

And it was strange, this feeling. Because it wasn't quite the fear that he remembered from a week or so ago. But it was something close to it.

The brain was amazing, the way it could adapt and create new neural pathways to compensate for damaged ones.

Worm regarded Mordechai and coughed a few times into the bicep of his good arm. "That motherfucker was crazy. You were right for handling that."

"*Pikuach nefesh*," the boy said.

"The fuck?"

"It means 'do no harm.' The preservation of life is the most important thing. People were being hurt." The boy looked at the Rebbe's body and gulped. "I had to do something."

"Oh yeah! You did something." Worm started coughing and had trouble stopping this time.

Mordechai looked like he was about to cry, but Worm wasn't paying attention. Something was happening.

Worm's vision began to fade, dissolving into a bleeding, gray watercolor painting. He felt lightheaded. It was like someone had tightened a belt around his lungs. He fell to his knees and tipped over onto the floor of the Rebbe's inner sanctum. On the floor with the Rebbe's body and Oloman's Toomp's body and the Golem's body and the golden pieces of the William Donald Schaefer and so much blood. "Aw man," he said.

"What's wrong?" Mordechai asked.

"It's not supposed to be like this."

"What isn't?"

"She said it isn't supposed to hurt," Worm said, pounding his chest, coughing and spitting blood. The gray watercolor painting was gone, replaced by a darkness not quite complete, but a darkness like the disposable sunglasses Dr. Osman had given him at the hospital. The one Toomp had snatched off his face. Everything was dark now, but he could still see the silhouette of the boy. The pattern of the hexagon ceiling above him. The lumpy shapes of the bodies he lay on the ground with.

"Who is *she*?"

"That fine-ass doctor. She said it wouldn't hurt. She said it would just happen."

Worm could no longer see. The boy was speaking to him, he knew this, but he couldn't understand what he was saying. The words were muffled, as if all the treble had been pulled out of the mix.

The mix of his brain. Where everything was bass now. His heartbeat was an 808 drum kick in his head. The blood pumping through his veins were muffled hi-hats, chopped and screwed, the pitch of their strikes lowered until they no longer resembled the sound of closed cymbals.

He focused on the snare. There had to be a snare. When it came, it sounded more like a floor tom because the pitch had been lowered as well.

Everything was low now.

Everything was completely dark.

Worm wondered if what the Sweet Breath hallucination had said was true. Not the part about there being no afterlife. Because that didn't matter. It mattered what you did when you were here. But he wondered about the hopelessness part. About the trying to make the world a better place part. And how the Sweet Breath hallucination–which was a part of his subconscious which meant a part of him believed this too–said nobody tried because nobody could. Nobody could change anything. And the smart ones knew that.

But that was the direction he was going after he got out of the hospital, and after he got out of prison before that.

Trying.

Had he gone into the situation with one bullet and shot at the right thing?

He would never find out. Worm died on the floor of the inner sanctum, joining the bodies of others who believed that they, too, were doing what was right.

"P.H. Park Heights, cold days, dark nights / start fights, bar fights, if one fight, we all fight"

- Lenwood

32

MORDECHAI WALKED DOWN PARK Heights Avenue, wiping the Rebbe's blood off on his trousers.

He worried for the Rebbe. Would he still have a place in *Olam HaBa*? After all he had done? Mordechai had been raised to believe that the sum of the father's deeds did not end at death. Mordechai had no father. The Rebbe was the closest thing to one. Could that mean something? Was it not true that the deeds and *zechuyot* of the son were reflective of the upbringing the father gave him? That *he* could spend the rest of his life performing *mitzvot* to make up for what his father had done?

The Rebbe had practically raised him. Perhaps he could be a better person. It would reflect well on the Rebbe.

He passed a comic book store and peered through the window at the images strobing across the flat screens. One of the televisions had a display in front of it–a small table with a black book propped up on a stand in the center of it. The title of the book was *Howl*.

A placard in front of the book read:

Howl, *the animated film. Based on the novel by E. Rathke.*

After being banished by the only people they have ever known, a man and woman wander the forest of towering mushrooms, where they meet Lady Agova, a giantess who has a job for them: help her hunt a vampire.

Set in a desolate postapocalyptic world where science and magic blend and reality itself twists and bends, where some attempt to grow a new world while others delve through the detritus of a shattered civilization, Howl *is a wild monster hunting ride.*

Mordechai was intrigued.

He loved cartoons and anime and manga and Adult Swim and–

Well, no. That wasn't quite right. He had never experienced any of these things. But he had seen them in fleeting glimpses, in shop windows like this one, or on flyers littered in the streets of Baltimore.

But he thought he might like them.

He watched the cartoon images on the screen strobe and blink, the neon colors dancing across the reflection of his eyes in the storefront glass. A massive, bald woman with pale skin wearing an ankle-length white coat buttoned all the way up to her neck swung a sword nearly as big as herself and lobbed off the head of some kind of wolf creature. Her scalp was tattooed with criss crossed scars that looked like thick centipedes crawling across her skull.

The animated film looked interesting. Mordechai thought that he might enjoy watching something like this. He fingered the bloody *tzitzit* that hung at his sides.

If he wanted to enjoy this cartoon, that would be fine. He could still be a good person. One had nothing to do with the other. The boy told himself that *mitzvot* done in memory of a person assists their soul in ascension. Something had gone wrong with the Rebbe. There was no *HaMoshiach*. And if there was, it was not him. And who was the Rebbe to say that he was, and take matters into his own hands?

He had been sick. And Mordechai had helped so many others by stopping him from that madness. His beloved Rebbe would not suffer in *Gehenom*. Mordechai would be the living proof of this.

The boy walked inside the comic book store.

To the people of Baltimore, thank you for your warmth and hospitality. Your kindness and willingness to share your stories and perspectives has been invaluable.

ABOUT THE AUTHOR

DAVID SIMMONS LIVES IN Baltimore with his wife and daughter.

Visit brokenriverbooks.com for our full catalogue.

Thank you for picking up this title.

Printed in the USA
CPSIA information can be obtained
at www.ICGtesting.com
LVHW022352220124
769680LV00045B/1636